Marji's Books

Grime Fighter Series

Grime Beat

Grime Wave

Grime Spree

Grime Family

Grime & Punishment

Heath's Point Suspense

Counter Point

Breaking Point

Boiling Point (coming soon)

Flash Point (coming soon)

Dallas Duets Clean Billionaire Romance

Ain't Misbehaving

Cry Me a River (coming soon)

Puttin' on the Ritz (coming soon)

Grime Beat

Grime Fighter Mystery
Book #1

Marji Laine

Grime Beat
Second Edition
© 2019 Marji Laine
ISBN: 978-1-944120-91-7

Faith Driven Book Production Services
Find out more about the author: *Marji Laine.com*
Or email her at: *AuthorMarjiLaine@gmail.com*

Printed in the United States of America.

For his constant support,
I dedicate this debut novella
to my patient, sweet hubby who
encourages me to indulge in
the desires of my heart!

*"He delivered us from such a deadly peril,
and He will deliver us.
On Him we have set our hope that
He will deliver us again."
II Corinthians 1:10*

Chapter One

Dani Foster edged into the parking lot of her friend's apartment complex. She roamed the three rows of cars, searching for her friend's Nissan in the ebbing daylight. Not a white sedan in the bunch. Parking near the center of the lot, she eyed the second-floor apartment.

If only Tasha would answer her phone. Dani had left a zillion texts and messages. Yet her calls were still answered with that same out-of-character recording. "I've gone dark. Deal with it."

The girl everyone dubbed "Sunshine" would never be so callous. Dani pictured her friend in her mind. Natasha Sanderson had a vivid smile, an enormous mane of blonde curls, and the enthusiasm of a perpetual cheerleader.

And the dependability of a postman.

That girl never missed work. Never. *Oh God, please don't let anything happen to Tasha.*

She parked in a spot and started to grab her sweater. Near sunset in mid-January, she'd normally need it, but a southern breeze had kept the weather warm since Christmas.

Dani left the layer behind and rushed up the stairs to the second-floor apartment. "Tasha, are you in there?" She knocked on her door. How many times over the past four months had she climbed those same steps? Usually with a big bag of chips for Tasha's delicious chili con queso.

She eyed the welcome decoration that hung beside the door and absently adjusted the burlap material on the bow. The knots in Dani's stomach that had initially formed over the tense conversation they'd shared on Friday tightened further. She pushed the door buzzer several times. An annoying sound, but not loud enough to her way of thinking. If only she'd been able to reach her during the weekend, to clear the air between them.

Instead, her concern turned to full-fledged worry from Tasha's silence. With her no-show this morning, that knot from the weekend threatened a stranglehold around her throat. *Help me find her, Lord.*

She pounded the cheap wood. The top edge gave a little with each contact. The lock held, but it wouldn't take much to break through. She called out again.

The door across the landing opened, and what must have been Hulk's sister advanced from within. "You wanna can that racket?"

Dani took a step backward. Then another. "Sorry. I'm looking for my friend who lives here. Have you seen her or heard anything from this place?" She laid her hand against Tasha's door.

The woman scowled and reentered her apartment.

"Does that mean no?" Dani clapped her hand over her mouth. Talking without thinking was going to get her belted one of these days. Probably would have at this point if the woman had heard her sarcasm.

She turned back to the door to knock again but halted, her hand in mid-pound, and eyed the closed door of the neighbor. No sense in inviting further conflict.

Maybe she could get in through the window?

The blinds were drawn and the room beyond dark. Dani tried to work her nails into the crack at the bottom of the metal strip, but it wouldn't budge.

She pressed her lips together. She wasn't about to give up. There had to be some way to find out what was going on. Especially with the ugly images that were starting to take root in her mind.

She trotted down the steps and around to the side of the building, looking toward the second floor. Blinds drawn at one window and frosted glass in the bathroom kept the interior secret. A hollow space grew in her chest.

She couldn't go home now. She'd never sleep. Not with the images of Tasha hurt or sick trolling around in her imagination. She walled against worse scenarios. Something had happened. That much was clear.

I know You know what's going on, Father. And I know You don't have to tell me. But could you please take care of Tasha, right now? And let me find some way to help her?

Part of her Bible reading from a few weeks back revisited her mind. "I will not leave you comfortless." The rest of the verse eluded her, but that part gave her the encouragement to keep searching. She wasn't alone.

She skirted to the back, sticking to the shadows. A little dog from the apartment under Tasha's started yapping. Sounded like a terrier. A sliding patio door opened, and Dani froze. This wasn't the type of companionship she needed right now. The barking volume increased, and the door slid into place with a click, leaving the dog scratching at the high patio fence.

Dani retreated several steps into the landscape, eying the enclosure. That really was a high wooden fence. Looked sturdy. She glanced to the top floor. The upper level held more of a balcony with a waist-high rail and pickets. And she could reach the bottom of them from the top of the lower porch.

She moved to the next apartment. Same structure here. And no animals. The loud-mouth next door was still throwing a fit, but at this angle its owners wouldn't see Dani if they looked out their patio door.

This was worth a try.

Backing up several feet, she took a running jump to the top edge of the wooden fence. The lifting and toting she did at work paid off. She pushed her arms straight over the rail, anchored there like a gymnast on a bar, and peered through the open drapes of the unit. The apartment appeared vacant. No lights, and no furniture.

She glanced at the whirling ball of black and brown fluff in the porch next door. Hard to believe so much noise came from such a tiny thing.

She swung her legs to catch one foot on the top of the rail and used the false stones at the side of the building for balance. Standing, she wrapped her hands around the bottom of the pickets on the upper floor.

The warm day had mocked her with visions of an early spring. Now, a chilled breeze with the smell of a cold, January rain caught her long bangs and sent a shiver across her shoulders. Served her right for leaving her sweater in the car.

She inched over to the farthest point and climbed to the next level as soundlessly as possible, using the rock facing. Reaching the porch next to Tasha's, she hugged the corner. This unit wasn't empty or dark. A couple of boys lay on their stomachs with some sort of metal machines fighting on the TV in front of them. It could be worse; the TV could be near the patio door, and they'd be looking right at her. Or it could've been Hulk's sister's apartment.

Knowing any minute, the kids could turn

around, she shuffled across the narrow rail. She took a giant step across to her friend's balcony and held onto the roof. Sunset orange streaked the sky. And she still had to get herself down.

Later.

First, she had to check on Tasha. Keeping a firm hold on the edge of the eave, she ducked her head to find drapes completely covering the closed door. Blah. She'd hoped to at least find the curtains cracked. They'd always been wide open whenever she visited, showing a stunning view of a little park and the rest of the complex on the other side.

She leaned forward and hopped off the rail. The sliding door was secure, and no lights showed through or around the curtains. Dani knocked against the glass. The sound echoed through the interior, and the dog beneath her upped his volume another decibel.

No response. This had been a waste of time. A patio chair next to her leaned against the wall. She righted and straightened it to be parallel with the rail. Moving forward, she leaned against the wooden beam and scanned the brown grass beneath her. What now? With all of her knocking, Tasha surely heard her. If she was there. Unless…

The line of thought she'd refused to entertain poured through her mind and iced her spine. She put her palms over her eyes. Would this place be the next crime scene she had to clean up, with the blood and ruin belonging to her dear friend instead of a tragic stranger?

She wiped her eyes hard. No. Tasha was fine. Just an unexpected trip. Or a new job opportunity. Goodness knew she could find a better environment in which to work. Surely, some hint of where she'd gone was inside the apartment. There had to be. If only Dani could find a way to get in there.

People like Tasha didn't just disappear.

But then, hadn't Dani done the exact same thing—left without a word or explanation? Had any of her friends tried to find her? She shook the troubling thoughts away. No reason to revisit that. Tasha couldn't be experiencing the disaster Dani had.

Besides, her friend couldn't keep a secret if she tried. If she had any, they wouldn't have stayed hidden for long. Especially since Dani was practically her only friend here. With both of them arriving in Dallas about the same time, they had bonded like sisters, often together at her place or

Dani's. They always got along. Always agreed. Even finished one another's sentences. And that fact made Friday's argument even more disconcerting.

Wait. Didn't Tasha have a skylight in her kitchen? Clear glass even. And she often propped it open to cool her home. Dani climbed back onto the corner of the porch rail. Using the rocks as a brace, she stood and peered over the edge of the soft incline. Sure enough, the remains of the sunset reflected off the glass about halfway up incline.

She planted her hands on the roof and lifted until her knee was firm on the edge. She thought to scramble up like a playground slide, but the shingles cut into the palms of her hands as she crept toward the glass. Though she was likely ruining her black jeans, the climb got easier the higher she went. Good thing she'd left her hair in a bun.

Upon reaching the skylight, she gasped. "Oh my gosh." Dani's shadow took out some of the illumination filtering in, but the empty refrigerator offered enough on its own.

Cans, pots, broken glass, and dishes covered the kitchen floor. Several cabinets next to it appeared as empty as the fridge. Likely their contents littered the beige tile along with the broken milk jug, smashed eggs, and a decimated loaf of bread.

What happened? She tried to peel the window from the frame. She didn't remember it ever being locked, but if it wasn't, it was much heavier than it looked. Much more than a normal window.

After two torn nails and a scratched fingertip, she finally accepted defeat. There was no way she'd be getting into the apartment without actually breaking something. And she wasn't prepared to go that far. Yet. She scanned the edges of light but couldn't make out any details beyond what sat directly in front of the fridge. The pantry and stove area cowered in deep shadows. Someone could even have been standing there looking at her, and she wouldn't have known.

Creepy thought. She backed away. If only she'd brought the flashlight from her car. Turning over, she sat and focused on the last hints of light on the horizon. Speaking of needing a flashlight …

Sirens sounded in the far distance. From her vantage point, a good part of the suburb spread out before her. Could have been a pleasant view if she wasn't so torn on what to do next.

She slid down on the roof, likely making her behind look just as bad as her knees. She needed a way… uh, down. Dani's throat went dry as the realization of her plight took hold.

Yikes. How had she come all this way? Resisting the urge to dig her fingernails into the shingles, she scooted back up. Going down from a climb had always been the scariest part. How was she supposed to navigate the descent in pitch black? Okay, not pitch, but dark enough to make getting back to solid ground impossible.

The sirens neared. Several of them from the sound of things. She scanned the horizon for a flame. Too dark to spot any smoke. The cloudless, moonless dusk illuminated nothing, but whirling lights appeared on the main thoroughfare not far from her. Police SUVs, ambulance, ladder truck. Must be something big going on somewhere.

They turned in to the lot next to her.

Oops.

The thought occurred that she might have better luck on the other side of the roof. Before she could move that direction, a spotlight found her. Someone with a bullhorn cleared his throat. "Miss, stay where you are. Lift your hands and keep them up."

She obeyed. What had she gotten herself into this time? She'd been ordered to maintain a low profile. Stay out of sight. Don't stir up trouble. Yet here she was in the thick of it all again.

Mere minutes passed before the top of a ladder clunked against the roof. The dog below went berserk. His barking probably earned the call to the police. Beasty ball of fluff.

The vague image of a policeman appeared. "Don't move, Miss. You are covered. Are you armed?"

What? Covered. Did that mean he had a gun? "Of course not." She didn't even have her phone with her.

The cop shined a flashlight into her eyes. "Scoot to your right."

She slowly lowered her hands and shoved her bottom across the harsh surface several times.

He kept the light trained on her. "Do you live in this complex?"

"No, I was looking for my friend. She lives in the apartment just below us but she's disappeared." She had as far as Dani could tell. "Someone wrecked her place." She stopped and lifted her hands again.

He lowered his light and looked back the way he had come. "Looks like she's okay." Then, he descended, leaving her there.

"Wait, you can see the wreck yourself..." Wasted effort. And her arms were beginning to chill, even with her long-sleeved tee shirt.

Less than a minute passed before a fireman's helmet rose above the edge of the roof. "Just stay put and we'll get you down." He kept coming and stepped onto the roof. An older guy with a nice face.

"Meow?" Dani mustered a half giggle.

"Excuse me?"

"I figure you usually work with cats stuck in trees. Thought a good meow might make you feel at home." She smiled.

The man didn't bite.

She sighed and cleared her throat. So much for finding humor in strained situations. "Can I put my hands down, now?

He nodded. "Are you hurt?"

"No, sir, but I'm better at going up than down." Dani pointed to the skylight. "See, I was worried about my friend. She's missing."

He stepped up the roof and peered through the glass. "Seems there's a reason to worry." He patted her shoulder. "Why don't we tell the fellows at the bottom about it after we get you back to firm ground?"

Another helmet appeared at the edge of the roof. The first guy guided her onto the ladder and helped her get her balance.

She clung to one post for a moment. *Don't look down.*

Despite her positive self-talk, she looked anyway. Epic fail.

The guy beneath her must have caught a whiff of her panic. "Keep your eyes on the rung in front of you. Just keep stepping. You won't fall."

Easy for him to say. He probably trained for hundreds of hours on these things. He helped her take the last long step to the base of the ladder where it rested on the back of the truck. Almost as tall as an eighteen-wheeler. She paused. "Quite a view from here."

The fireman came down behind her. "Not as good as the one you had up top, but it's safer down here."

With the first guy already on the pavement, she climbed down the back of the truck.

A cop took her by the upper arm. "I'm going to have to arrest you for trespassing, young lady."

He pulled her hands behind her back and snapped on handcuffs.

The cold metal dug into Dani's wrists. "Wait a minute. You don't understand."

The fireman who had helped her onto the ladder stepped close and said something to the cop, though his helmet blocked Dani's view of his face, and she couldn't hear anything more than a baritone mumble.

After the fireman walked away, the officer took her by the elbow. "I'm guessing, since you don't have any stolen items on you, that you weren't able to break in."

"Oh, I could've broken in, but I didn't want to break anything. I was more trying to see in." Wait, that didn't come out the way she meant. Her shoulder twitched into a spasm from the angle of her arm. She gritted her teeth.

"Really. Brings a new realm to window peeper I guess." He led her to an SUV with swirling lights. "Your name?"

Twisting her wrist against the cuff hurt like the dickens but relieved some of the pressure on her shoulder. "Dani Foster. But you have to help me. The place in there is trashed." She tried to point, making her shoulder ache again.

"It's none of your business how people keep their homes." He opened the back door.

"Didn't the fireman tell you about it?" She halted and spotted the engine as it roared to life and pulled away.

"He said it was messy, but there's nothing that proves you didn't create the vandalism yourself."

"Vandalism?" She was really in for it when her security agent got wind of this.

The policeman hesitated, but only for a moment. "If nothing else, lady, you're under arrest for trespassing. We'll see if there was a break-in."

"But there was. There had to be. Tasha's apartment was always neat." She squirmed as he tugged her toward the back seat.

"You know the resident? Maybe you had a fight and wanted to get back at her?"

"Yes, I mean no. I do know the resident. Tasha. Natasha Sanderson. That's what I'm trying to tell you. My friend is missing." Dani sighed. Finally, she'd gotten out the most important detail. Maybe he'd unlatch the horrible chains around her wrists.

"We'll check it out at the department."

"No. Please." She couldn't be arrested. The

records would uncover too many dangerous details.

He put his hand on her head and shoved her inside.

Grime Beat

Chapter Two

Upon arrival at the police station, Dani's escort pointed to a hard bench in the waiting room. "Sit there. I'll be back."

This couldn't be happening. Not now. Especially not here.

Lord, please, help me. What a mess. And she had no one to blame except herself and her stubborn insistence on trying to figure out what was going on with Tasha.

She eyed the exit across the room. Handcuffs would be rather noticeable on someone going out. The cop who brought her in stepped into her line of vision. "We aren't thinking of leaving so quickly, are we?"

Dani sighed and shifted in her seat. A desk to

her right was littered with papers and office paraphernalia. How could anyone stand to work in such a distracting environment?

The cop who was her escort opened one of the drawers, pulled out a notepad, and added it to the pile on the desktop.

Figured he was the owner of the mess.

She turned her disdain toward the entrance. A tall man, dark hair and broad shoulders, crossed the room. "Hey, I know him."

The cop turned around. "Really?"

"Yes. Jay Hunter. He's a crime scene specialist. I work with him." Well, she cleaned up after him often enough. Usually once or twice a week.

"You? Work with Jay?" The man leaned against a rickety metal desk and scratched his bald head.

"Ask him. He'll vouch for me." At least, she thought he would. They'd never been chummy, but since the third partner on her cleaning team was his best friend, she saw him often enough.

The older cop narrowed his gaze.

"I'm just worried about my friend. Jay knows her, too." Not that he spoke with either of them very often, except to make sure he hadn't left any evidence behind.

That man was nothing if not serious about doing his job.

The cop pointed a finger at her. "Stay."

"Woof." It popped out before she could think to bite it off.

With a smirk the officer strode through the room, maneuvering between movable walls and other uniforms. He leaned in at the entrance of one of the nearest cubes. "Gotta a lady here that says you'll vouch for her."

She couldn't hear Jay's response, but the other cop's baritone barreled above the humming of machines and conversations around the room. "No, she ain't a prostitute. Said her name is Dani Foster. Caught her peeping through an apartment skylight."

She imagined the look of horror on Jay's face. If he didn't already think she was nuts from her ridiculous comments when they met on the job, he would now. And she couldn't help her nervousness when she was around him. Tall, dark, and handsome didn't do a smidge of justice to the man.

The cop rejoined her at the bench. "He'll be here in a minute. I told him you'd wait."

She rolled her eyes. Cop humor. She'd grown up with it at almost every meal. She huffed.

"I wouldn't look that horse in the mouth if I were you." The cop didn't connect that she was exasperated with him, not Jay, but she wouldn't enlighten him.

Besides, Jay was hardly a horse. Tall and muscular, yes. But with short black hair, an easy smile, and a gorgeous permanent tan. Native American in his background, probably. He had a good sense of humor, too, when he wasn't concerned that he'd made some mistake.

One time in the four months she'd worked for Kellerman's, he'd missed a tiny bit of evidence that no investigator would have seen. And the pieces hadn't meant anything anyway. But it irked the tar out of him.

"Can I at least get these off?" She stood and turned her hands toward the heavy-set officer.

He unlocked the bindings. "You say your friend is missing? When did you last see her?"

She sat again, rubbing her wrists. "Friday. She was supposed to be at work today, but she never showed, and that's completely odd for her. She's always on top of things."

"So today is the first day you've missed her."

He took out an iPad mini and tapped it a few times.

"Not really. I mean, I've been trying to talk to her since Saturday morning. We talk almost every day."

He stroked his finger across the glass. "Uh-huh. You say her apartment looks messy?"

"Trashed, like it had been searched. From what I saw, the entire contents of the kitchen were strewn across the floor."

He typed with two fingers while he held the pad in his other hand. "And how old is the woman, Tasha, right?"

"Twenty-five. She's studying for her law degree."

"Hmph." He typed some more. "Coloring?"

"Blonde. Blue eyes. Light skin. About five foot-three or four and slender. You know, fit."

"Can you tell me about other friends, pastimes, or places she'd frequent?"

"She loves garage sales, antique stores, and pawn shops. And resale stores like Goodwill. She's always treasure hunting in places like that. As far as I know, she doesn't have any friends. Besides me and Tyrone. We all work together. She has an aunt who lives out in East Texas, but she's moved into a senior living center." She was rambling. She shut her mouth and rolled her lips between her teeth.

"Could she be visiting her aunt?"

"I called the center. The receptionist said that Aunt Dodie hasn't had any visitors."

"I'm not sure your concerns will be enough to warrant a search of her home. Not at this point anyway."

Jay came over from his cube in a relaxed saunter. A smirk highlighted his strong jawline.

"I hear this lady had a bit of trouble, Kirkland?" He patted the other cop's shoulder.

"We haven't been able to confirm breaking and entering. So just a trespass."

He released a heavy exhale. Had he really thought she'd done something criminal? Well, more criminal than just climbing on a roof. She stroked a finger over her sore wrists. Welts had started rising.

He eyed her hands. "Trespass usually rates a citation. Why cuffs?"

The older officer tilted his head. "Are you questioning my response to a serious situation, Hunter? Because if you are, you can take a formal complaint to the captain, but you'll be getting a black mark on your own record."

Jay raised his palms. "I'm not doubting your action. I'm curious as to what provoked it. Was she belligerent?"

"Sitting right here." Once again, Dani's big-mouth curse rose up. Thankfully, Jay didn't pause, and neither man seemed to notice her comment.

"Was she abusive or try to fight and put you or the firemen in danger? Maybe she clammed up, refusing to respond to your questions or explain what she was doing on the roof?" Jay tucked his forefingers into the front pockets of his slacks. "If so, I'm not sure I want to do any vouching."

Kirkland lifted her arm. "Maybe we should just stick her in a cell for the night and sort it all out tomorrow."

Dani stood. "Wait, wait, wait. I didn't do any of those things. I did exactly as you instructed. I told you about my missing friend. Aren't you going to file a missing person report or something?"

"Your friend is missing?" Jay turned his dark gaze on her with a hint of a wrinkle between his brows.

"Tasha. I haven't been able to reach her since Friday."

He took Dani's elbow out of Kirkland's grasp. "Thanks. I've got it from here."

She hesitated and straightened the inbox to square it with the corner of the desk. Jay's tug on her arm got her moving again.

The older man reddened. "See to it that you do." He scowled in Dani's direction.

Jay hurried Dani out the door. Any tiny detail or halfway decent excuse could change Kirkland's mind. Hopefully, the man had not been too angry. The last thing he needed was a derogatory report to his supervisor. Even over something little like this.

Once outside, he slowed. "What did you do to Kirkland?"

Her eyes widened as she turned toward him. "Nothing. Not to him."

He raised his eyebrow in her direction. Maybe he should have learned more about her circumstances before he stepped in and put his reputation on the line.

"Not to anybody." She stared at the cement in front of her as she walked.

He regretted his suspicions. Poor thing. Usually she had a mischievous smile and a quip to share. But now, even with the disarming blush to her cheeks, she looked plain miserable.

"You want to tell me about Tasha?" Jay opened the passenger door of his Charger. "Oh, hang on." He grabbed a Whataburger bag out of the seat. He shoved some stray napkins from the floor into it and scooped up his Bible and a sweaty tee shirt.

"There you go." He watched her climb in and shut the door behind her. It had been a long time since he'd had a lady in his car. Not that a police car, even an unmarked one, was such a great chick-magnet. He'd always had that excuse to fall back on whenever anyone like Tyrone messed with him about not dating.

He deposited his stuff in the trunk, shoving his spare-clothes duffle into the deepest corner and squaring the first aid box with his large case of tools for crime scene assessment. That done, he climbed into the driver's seat and adjusted his leather-covered steering wheel. Why did he suddenly feel first-date awkward? "Shall I call you Peeping Tom? Or maybe Peeping Tammy?" He shot her a half-grin, attempting to cover for his lame attempt at humor. The engine roared into action, and he made his way out of the lot.

Dani pulled the knot out of the back of her hair releasing it to fall around her shoulders in a chocolate swirl. He'd do better to keep his eyes, and mind, on the road.

"I wasn't a peeping anything." She leaned one arm on the passenger door and anchored it against her temple. "Tasha didn't show up today. You've seen how dependable she is."

Jay took the ramp to I-35. Yeah, he'd never noticed her missing from the team. "How is it I haven't heard from Tyrone about this?" Wouldn't his best friend have called him?

"I don't know what's up with him. He thought all day that she would show up."

"Had he spoken with her?"

She shook her head and looked out the passenger window. A flash of neon sped by on this darker side of town. "But Tasha and I are a lot closer than her and Tyrone."

He'd seen evidence of what Dani said and thought they'd been childhood friends before they corrected him. Tyrone called them the Superglue Twins because of their quick, tight bond.

His radio blared a 41-11. He turned the

volume down. "She didn't show, and you were worried."

"So, after Tyrone and I finished the job today, I stopped by her home to check on her."

He shrugged. "Ever think of calling?"

She turned and cocked her head to the side with a sarcastic expression. "Oh, you mean like all o' them city folk do on them commercial thingys." Her voice carried a high-pitched twang.

Cute accent. He cut his eyes in her direction.

She dropped the attitude. "Been at it since Saturday morning." She told him about the voice mail recording. "She must have changed it this weekend. Before Saturday morning, it was her usual, perky self. It's so… odd."

"Like climbing on the roof of a two-story building?" He took the exit to a busy intersection and went north. "I still can't believe you got all the way up there."

She explained about the porch rails and the rock edgings that gave her footing. "I've always been good at climbing… up anyway."

"How did you expect to get down in the dark?" He stopped at another intersection. Now after seven o'clock, the streets had emptied out considerably.

"I didn't think about that. And it wasn't dark when I started." She turned her brown eyes toward him.

Her gaze mesmerized him for a nanosecond. Focus. The light turned green, but the pickup in front of him remained.

Jay tapped his horn and received a rude gesture for his trouble.

"You going to let him get away with that?"

"I'm not a patrolman. Never have been. Besides, what could I arrest him for? Inappropriate use of fingers?"

"It's disrespectful."

"Yeah, but he doesn't know I'm a cop." Of course, that wouldn't have changed anything except to make the driver's reaction worse perhaps. "So back to Tasha being missing. I'm assuming she wasn't inside her apartment."

"I don't know. I couldn't get in. She wasn't in the kitchen, but the floor looked like it held the contents of the entire room."

His mind pictured the scene. "The refrigerator? The cabinets?"

"Food, dishes, cookware, drinks. Everything was on the tile and most of it broken or opened. Someone was looking for something."

He slowed through one of the suburbs that insisted even busy streets have a speed limit of no higher than thirty. Driving so slow physically pained him, but not as much as getting pulled over would. "What gave you that conclusion?" He'd seen Dani's precision in her work. She had a sharp mind to go along with her mildly sarcastic wit.

"Ice cream."

Huh? He looked around. Did she want some? Office furniture wholesalers, a carpet store, a larger home-furnishings store, a printing company—nothing that would inspire ice cream. A McDonald's came into view. He turned on his right blinker. "You want ice cream?"

"No." She gave him a puzzled look. "The ice cream is what made me think someone was searching."

He needed to give his head a swift shake to get his ears in tune with his brain. Obviously, he wasn't hearing or processing correctly.

Or the girl who shared his car was a loon.

"You didn't see it. The ice cream didn't just melt out of the round container. It had been shoveled out. Large puddles of mint chocolate chip splatted on the floor like the half-gallon had been clawed through."

"I see." Though he wasn't completely convinced.

"And her full loaf of bread. The slices had been pulled out and scattered about the floor. Why else would anyone do that?"

He didn't want to hazard a suggestion.

"I know you two are close, but maybe she needed to get away. You know, take a break." He stopped at another light and took the opportunity to use his mounted tablet to punch up the address of Dani's encounter on the rooftop.

She leaned her head back against the seat. "We did argue on Friday. But she always calls her aunt every Sunday, right after church. Like clockwork. Doesn't even eat lunch until she talks to her." She rocked her head in his direction. "The receptionist there said she didn't call yesterday. Not at all. Tasha would never have skipped something like that. Her aunt is the only family she has left."

"But y'all argued?"

"It was strange. She was cold. I thought I might have said something to offend her." The corners of her mouth turned down and she glanced at him. "I have a bad habit of speaking first and regretting later."

"So I've heard." He chuckled. "Did y'all settle things?"

"No. I still don't know what I did. She said she'd call me, but I didn't hear from her." She sniffed and turned her eyes back toward the darkened window.

"You gave Kirkland a description?"

She nodded, rubbing at something on the edge of his window. "I don't think he took it very seriously, though."

"Doesn't matter. The missing person's report will go out. Do you have a picture of her?"

"At home, but I need my car first."

He turned left at the next light. "Tasha's place isn't in the best part of town." He eyed the old brick of the empty buildings that lined the street in the suburban oldtown. "You're lucky that a finger of the city of Dallas extends up here."

"I guess Dallas's strange city limits make emergencies hard."

"Yeah, but at least the different departments work together pretty well." Jay smirked. "Though it's unlikely any of them would take my vouching for you. Good thing your location fell within jurisdiction of my unit."

She looked at him. "Let's make one thing

perfectly clear. I didn't fall at all." A quick smiled graced her lips.

He laughed outright and pulled into Tasha's lot. Quiet and way too dark. "I'll follow you back to your place."

"You don't have to do that. I can just email them in."

"If you'd made the report yourself, you could. But since Kirkland wrote it up, you don't have access to it, so you can't edit it or add the images." He wouldn't add that Kirkland's computer skills weren't the best.

He scanned the lot as she moved toward her car. Better than watching her walk away from him in her tight jeans. Even the long-sleeved, gray tee shirt she wore didn't detract from her obvious beauty. How was a girl so smart, pretty, and with such a fun personality still single?

He thought she was single. Maybe he should spend a little time looking her up in the databases.

About ten minutes later, he trailed her into a complex. Not quite as dark as Tasha's, but Dani lived on the backside of the place. A large field provided what was probably a lovely view, but not much security.

She parked under a carport and climbed from

her car, tugging on a sweater. She swung her lengthy hair over one shoulder and tucked a strand behind her ear.

Way cute. But he dared not enjoy the sight too much. He had no time for women. Any women.

Much to Tyrone and his wife's dismay. He parked in an open spot, emerged from his car, and half-sat on the corner of his hood.

Dani dashed up to the second level swallowed by the night. A minute later the lights in her apartment illuminated the full staircase. She came back into view, jogging down the steps. "Here they are. They're the only prints I have of her."

One of her and Dani. Another at a pool party with Tasha in a summer dress.

Dani stepped backward. "Thanks for your help tonight. I'm glad you were there. I'd be sitting in a cell otherwise."

"Mmm. Not likely. If no one presses charges for something like trespassing, there's no real reason to arrest you. I'm kinda surprised Kirkland brought you to the station in the first place." He returned to the driver's side of the car, opened the door, and slipped the photos into a hidden pocket above his car visor. "Maybe he was just trying to scare you."

"It worked." She took a few steps toward her apartment.

He paused with his elbows propped on the top of his car and his door. "Listen, you sit on this for a couple of days and let me check a few things out." He couldn't let her start making noises around the department, especially after he vouched for her. And anyone who would climb a building wouldn't likely stop investigating. "I bet Tasha will be back by then, but if she isn't, I'll have some answers for you."

She turned back. "Okay." Her tone sounded tentative, and her wrinkled brow looked unconvinced.

If she kept the promise for twenty-four hours, he'd be lucky

Chapter Three

Finally, blood no longer splayed the walls and windows. Dani worked with a squeegee to make the last room in the tiny living area sparkle. She could do that much for the poor woman who lost her son over the weekend.

The squeak of the tool on the glass pinched a nerve. Like fingernails on slate. She stiffened and resisted the urge to rub her sore shoulders, especially in front of her boss.

Frank Durmondo leaned through the open entry from the tiny kitchen. He held a handkerchief over his mouth. "You done yet?" With Tasha gone, Frank had been assigned to play the third on their team, though all he'd done was stand around and complain. She never thought she'd be happy that the man was her team's leader, but after witnessing his lousy effort at being a team member, she'd never gripe about him arriving at the last moment again.

She shoved a stained throw-pillow into the hazardous material container on her cart. "Almost." The Haz-Mat helmet she wore amplified her voice to her own ears.

"Well, hurry up."

Her missing partner sure delayed the process. Promise to Jay Hunter or not, she'd started calling her friend's cell again at dawn. Tasha never answered.

Frank caught her making yet another call just after they arrived at the tiny, gray box of a house. He threw a fit and threatened to take her phone away. "Most unprofessional."

As if he understood the concept.

Still, she'd better not attempt another call unless Frank left her alone for half a second. Which he hadn't, not even during their abbreviated lunch.

Knowing him, he'd actually try to make good on his threat, and she'd have to flatten him.

Tyrone excused his way through the door with the emptied carpet cleaner. Though the brownish-red grime had disappeared with his first pass, Kellerman Crisis and Trauma Cleaners promised a thorough cleaning. Always. The noisy machine revved when he flipped the switch. Gruesome work, but finally the evidence of the murder and the police presence had been erased from the walls, floors, and furniture.

Dani pushed away from the newly cleaned couch and took another swipe at the glass with the tool. She cringed at the sound that somehow pierced the moan of the whirring cleaner. She put the squeegee away and waved at Frank for his attention. "All clear."

She slipped her helmet off and smoothed her hair back. With a fresh, floral fragrance dusting the room, she could almost imagine she worked for a regular cleaning service. A normal job, instead of the gore of untimely death and the emotions that typically went along with such.

Her boss still blocked the doorway. She inched the metal cart in his direction and shouted over the machine noise. "You want to roll this out?"

He snorted and pushed through the entrance toward the back of the house. Probably going to collect from the victim's mom. The grime of the job rarely bothered her. Her dad had cured her of squeamishness with all of his cop stories told in vivid detail. But the heartless way Frank did business hit her from time to time. Especially his pinched smile when he announced a completed job by telling the bereft family members things were good as new.

Like de-staining carpet eliminated embedded scenes of a violent end or filled the void left behind. The images of red puddling on the plush cream rug pierced her memories. She shut her eyes and willed thoughts of that horror-filled day away.

Reliving her past endangered her line of work. She pushed the heavy tool carrier over the door facing of the clapboard home. Tyrone would have to help her carry the supplies down the warped steps. In an unsupervised moment, she slipped out of her yellow, disposable coveralls and inverted the suit into a plastic bag along with her cap and latex gloves. She tugged her phone from her jeans pocket.

No calls. No voice messages. No texts. Dani dialed Tasha's number and got the same recording she'd heard all weekend. If only she knew why. A beep sounded. "Girl, where are you? Call me. Really. I'm way past worried."

The noise from inside waned and Tyrone appeared, dragging the cleaner and wrapping up the cord. "Heard from Natasha?" He swung the heavy machine off the porch and landed it on the walkway with hardly a bump.

"Not a peep." Images of broken eggs and spoiled milk flitted through Dani's mind. She hadn't told Tyrone about last night's escapade. No need to get him riled at her.

But the man was worried, regardless of the way he tried to hide it. The typical broad smile that contrasted his gleaming teeth with his brown skin had been almost non-existent. And when he had used it, he hadn't stretched it wide enough to even show the teeth.

Her partner reached for the cart and took most of the weight while Dani guided it. He led her to the big, white box truck with the Kellerman name marching across the side in formal font. "Carla about chewed my ears off last night with one disastrous possibility after another."

Hearing about his wife's worries made the knot around her stomach tighten. Didn't he know she needed encouragement right now? Something like, *she'll be fine, and we'll laugh about this later.* Or maybe, *it's probably just a low phone battery.*

Not that she'd believe any shallow attempts, but it would be nice to hear them.

He dragged the floor cleaner down the sidewalk. "Likely not any worse than the poisonous thoughts you've been filling your mind with, I bet."

Dani paused at the ramp and thumbed through her emails. Nothing. "Something's happened. You know it, and I know it."

"It's strange. I'll give you that." He hoisted his machine up the ramp.

"Maybe we can drive past her place on the way back to the warehouse?" She had to get into that apartment. Had to be sure Tasha wasn't lying there with an empty look in her blue eyes. Ugh, if only she could keep the morbid images out of her mind.

She gave the cart a shove, and Tyrone pulled it up the ramp, securing it to the bed.

"I bet we could do that." His mouth spread into a fraction of his typical wide cocoa and ivory smile.

With Ty's help, she could find a way into Tasha's place. Pulling her hair out of the knot on her head, Dani thought through their last conversation on Friday. Tasha talked about doing a little treasure hunting—pawn-shopping and hitting some garage sales. Usually she invited Dani to join her, but not this time. For reasons still unknown.

Dani raked through her thoughts about Friday's job. Nothing special—a flooded lower floor. Waders, a water pump, and a couple of hours of polishing and drying left the owners happy. Well, until Frank converged on them. But that didn't explain Tasha's issues. Come to think of it, she'd been edgy from the beginning of the day.

"That's all for today, children." Her boss clomped across the porch in Ostrich boots. "I'll follow you back to the warehouse to unload and reset the stage for tomorrow's work." He tossed one tail of his green scarf over his shoulder. The man should've been in the theater.

Dani caught Tyrone's eye. So much for their planned detour.

Jay leaned against his Dodge and eyed the Meyer's small house from across the street. The pain that had lined the grieving mother's face stirred the deepest part of his heart. *God bless that poor woman.* At least he'd done what he could to ensure the killer went to jail.

Still, even though he was positive he hadn't missed any details at the scene, he had to stick around after the clean-up. Had to double check with Tyrone to put his mind at ease.

Dani came onto the porch and shed her protective gear. If she saw him, she gave no indication. But why should she? He'd been revisiting his crime scenes the entire time she'd worked for Kellerman's, and his purpose had never been to see her.

His phone vibrated. His partner. What did Cal want? "Can't a guy have some off-time?"

"Oh, so you're familiar with that idea? And you're not standing in front of your latest crime scene doubting every decision?" Cal knew him far too well.

"I think maybe it's time I had a new partner."

"Ha, like you could replace me, Buddy-o."

"I'll head home in a few minutes." Jay pocketed his phone and eyed the gray frame house. With three injured witnesses, he'd done more first aid than investigating when he'd arrived at the site. Not that there was much to investigate. The tiny place contained very little. Besides, the suspect was caught only a few blocks away with the drugs still on him and a deep gash in his leg.

Open and shut case.

Tyrone came out of the house. He and Dani packed the truck. Jay would call the man when they got done—like he always did—just to settle his mind that he hadn't erred.

And until a couple of weeks ago, the answer had always been no evidence to add. Jay still ached from the depressing conversation after the suicide when they had found items that he'd left behind.

That case, too, had seemed easy. At least until Tyrone and crew bagged several pieces Jay overlooked. Jewelry of some sort. Didn't turn out to be important, but he'd still missed it. Like an elephant sat in his crime scene, and he'd somehow not noticed.

Jay watched the duo across the street. That team was the best. If he had missed something, one of them surely caught it. And he'd find out before they turned the stuff in.

He just had to wait until they hit the road.

The boss exited the house, and Ms. Meyers

closed the front door behind him. Again, Jay lifted a prayer for the dead man's mom. If for no other reason, he'd continue his habitual visitations for the opportunity to pray for the survivors.

The white truck pulled away with the red Camaro following. Looked like Tasha didn't show again today. He wished he had more information on that girl, but her cell recording told the story. Gone dark. No digital trail whatsoever.

He watched their taillights for a second before climbing into his driver's seat. He tapped Tyrone's contact button and waited for the greeting. "So, Mr. Clean, how did you find things today?"

"Messy." Tyrone chuckled. "You boys sure do throw wicked parties."

Wicked was right. "And?"

"And you worry too much. What's the big deal if you left something behind? As long as somebody finds it, no problem."

"So I did?" His stomach dropped. How? What? He'd never make detective if he couldn't become a team supervisor. And that fantasy had no chance if he kept ignoring evidence.

"I didn't say that."

"I can't believe I'm slipping like this. How could something get by me in a house that small?"

"Relax, bro. Nothing surfaced. You're clean. But in all of the acreage you comb through over the period of a month, I'd think you could cut yourself a little slack."

Ha. Not if he wanted the supervisor spot that was opening. At 32, his dad was already sheriff. Things were different back then, but Jay should at least lead his own team by now. "Maybe next year. For now, it's one scene at a time." He wasn't the most qualified for the coming position. Cal had more experience, but he didn't want the job. "So Tasha's still a no show?"

"You noticed."

Tyrone was forever trying to set Jay up with different ladies. "Don't get any ideas. I'm just curious."

"Dani's about to bust out of her seat belt. I keep telling her people take off work all the time."

Likely Tyrone was downplaying for the benefit of the brunette beside him. "Let me talk to her." He waited while the phone was handed over.

Dani's smooth greeting followed. "Have you learned anything?"

"Not much. But it sounds like you haven't said anything about your fun last night to Tyrone."

"Haven't had the chance, but I will... I think.

No need to worry." Though her tone escalated up the scale a notch.

"Don't forget your promise."

She probably already had, but at least while she was working, he could count on her staying off of roofs.

"What about yours?" Her challenge sounded like trouble.

"You're going over there, aren't you?"

"Can't. Frank is following us back to the warehouse."

"Just as well. I'm still looking into things. And you need to let me. I'll send you an update tomorrow." He glanced at an irritation on his hand. How did he get a mosquito bite in the middle of winter? Even in North Texas those buggers should be little frosty spots on the concrete by now.

"I'm beginning to wonder just how good you are at your job." She hung up.

His neck stiffened. Her nerves and worry over her friend were talking. And he couldn't blame her. He had the same doubts. Maybe he should check out Tasha's home on his own.

Chapter Four

Tyrone's chatter succeeded in partly distracting Dani on the way to the warehouse. Still, every dip in the road reminded her of Tasha's "Whoops-i-daisy." What had happened to that girl?

"You hear me?" Coming to a stop light, Tyrone fully turned to stare at her.

"I'm sorry. I was thinking about Tasha."

He shook his head. "I have a feeling she'll turn up and be flattered and embarrassed that she caused you so much worry. But I was talking about Carla's birthday."

His wife's birthday? "What about it?"

"You promised to spend a little time with us. I want you and Carla to get to know each other better. Especially if Tasha's gone for a while. You need another female to talk to."

He was probably suggesting it for survival purposes. "I'm happy to celebrate with you guys. If you don't think it will be too awkward."

"She'll love it. I'm planning something for tomorrow night. You game?"

Dani nodded, plans already forming in her mind for this evening. Tasha's place was the only lead she had. By the time she'd finished her prep duties, Tyrone had already said goodbye. So much for using his skills or flat-out brawn to get into Tasha's apartment. Just as well. She'd hate to be responsible for getting Tyrone into more trouble than she'd been in the night before.

This time, things would be different. She'd go through the proper channels. Follow protocol. Even if she was ignoring her promise to Jay.

She arrived at the police station, and Kirkland directed her to the same bench she inhabited the night before. The man smirked and whispered to other cops.

She felt like she had bubblegum stuck in her hair, her skirt tucked into her tights, or her shoes on the wrong feet. Her dad's friends had always made her feel that way, too. Only at age twenty-eight, she no longer chewed bubblegum and never wore tights. She glanced at her shoes. Good there, too.

Her temper flared a bit, but she slapped a pleasant look on her face and stood. "Officer Kirkland, are you going to do a search of my friend's home or not?"

The men snickered and dispersed. A couple of them even came closer. She thought they were going to ask her some questions, get involved with the investigation, but they just sat at nearby desks.

"Simmer down, Miss Foster. I've inputted all of your friend's information on the National Database for Missing Persons. It would help to add a picture to the file."

"So, choose one and add it." Did he need her permission or something?

"Do you have some for me?"

"No... I..." She iced. Jay had them. He'd promised to turn them over. A couple of the cops were staring at her.

"The best way to find your friend is to have a picture of her. If you can't locate a photo, then you can pay an expert to have a composite drawn." He continued with what sounded like a long-winded sales pitch.

Did Jay forget? How could he? And now a whole day had been wasted when the cops should have been searching. Not to mention they were the only photos she had of Tasha—well, the only non-blurry ones. Now more than ever she wanted to get into that apartment. If for no other reason than to find another good picture of her friend. She turned on her heel and stomped out as loud as her Converse shoes allowed.

She drove directly to Tasha's home. Jay Hunter would be hearing about this. She trusted him. And this was police business, so he couldn't make the excuse that he was working.

Police or not, she'd get into that apartment this time. And she wouldn't be so loud as to upset the monstrous neighbor or the megaphoned mutt.

What did she have to help her get through the door? A credit card? That was old-fashioned, but still possible with the right type of lock. Only Tasha had a deadbolt. If it was engaged, the credit card wouldn't help at all. In fact, nothing would work besides a locksmith's kit or a crowbar.

Wait. A crowbar was in her trunk. And using the wedge and lever wouldn't make much noise.

She pulled into Tasha's lot. Since the temperature had plummeted, all of the cars crowded close to the building. She wrapped up in her coat and trotted to the trunk of the car.

She grabbed the crowbar from under the mat. A heavy-duty flashlight had shared the hole. That would be handy. Snatching it as well, she shut the lid and broke into a jog. The wind whipped her coat around behind her. Like a sail, it kept trying to jerk her off-course. And she had no hands left to pull it close and keep it under control. She leaned into the gale as she took the stairs.

When she reached the door, she halted. Was that a light? She started to knock when a beam, like from a flashlight, crossed the window next to the door. Her throat tightened. Someone was in there who wasn't supposed to be. Had the person who trashed the place returned?

And what should she do?

Not call the police. After last night, they'd likely arrest her just for being there again. She couldn't chance that. But she also couldn't let whoever was inside get away.

A strong gust blew through the walkway. Tasha's front door creaked slightly and moved in the breeze. Dani touched it and the wood gave under her pressure. She had a way in now. Setting down the crowbar, she shut her eyes and paused a moment to let them get accustomed to the dark. Alarms in her head screamed for her to return to her car, but she shut them out. Whoever was inside had no idea she was here. She just needed a look at him… or her.

She nudged the door and left it open in case she needed a quick exit. The fridge light still highlighted the kitchen, and the scent of rotting food filled the air. The hall to the back bedroom that Tasha used as her office and study was a solid black rectangle.

Dani crept up to the edge of the master entrance. The door was partly closed. She crossed the gap and peeked inside. Someone stood with his back to her, flipping through papers on Tasha's desk. She watched him a minute. Definitely a man with muscular shoulders.

She was an idiot for being in here. This guy could be a killer for all she knew.

At that moment, a gale blew through the landing dogtrot. The front door slammed shut. Dani jumped back a couple of feet, and something fell over in the bedroom. The man would come out to investigate.

Her heart pulsing in her ears, she darted into the black studio. She stumbled over something on the floor but caught herself. A destroyed shelf unit cluttered half of the room. Dani could barely make out ripped up books, files, and desk supplies tangled in the destruction. She crawled in behind the mess with a full view of the hallway about the time the flashlight beam pierced the darkness.

The porch door was on her right. Even in the dark, she could always escape that way, if she had to.

Keeping her eyes peeled on the shadows, she spotted the man emerging from the bedroom. He shined his flashlight around the living room, then in her direction. She froze, but the destroyed shelf unit hid her. He went into the kitchen. Footsteps crunched on the glass. When he came out, he once again shined the light into the room she inhabited, but not down on her level. He made his way in her direction. She lowered her head so he wouldn't catch a reflection from her eyes.

God help me get out of this stupid situation I've stuck myself in.

The figure played his light over her camouflage. It brushed by her. He couldn't have spotted her. She hazarded a glance. The light seemed to pause on the ground when the man reached the doorway. He played the light to the other side of the room as he entered. Stepping in that direction, he kept the beam on the ground.

A torn chair, a toppled stool, a shattered TV. Had anything been left intact? The possibility of finding a picture of Tasha had already been slim. Now, that prospect hinged on her avoiding the creep who advanced way too close to her.

If he raised his light a couple of feet, he'd have a clear view of her, but just as he reached that point, he turned and scanned the doorway and the center of the room again. His calf was within arm's length. She held her breath.

Turning his back to her, he shot his light at the floor and pulled an edge of the drapes away from the patio door. Now was her only opportunity. She gripped her flashlight with both hands, stood and brought it down hard on the man's head.

He flinched. His light hit the floor. He half-turned in her direction before he fell.

Jay Hunter crumpled at her feet.

Jay's head ached. He turned to the side, but the room toppled.

"Whoa there, big fella." Someone pushed him back to center. At least he thought it was center.

He opened his eyes to dim light coming from behind him, the refrigerator. So that meant he was in the front room. How had he gotten here? And how long had he been out?

"You awake?" A dim figure queried with an East Texas accent. Fake if he was any judge.

"I'm awake." He moved to get up and found his hands bound together from wrists to mid-palm. His knees were pinched together as well. If he could manage to stand, he wouldn't go anywhere fast.

"What are you doing here?"

"Are you Tasha?" Sounded like the blonde. Sort of. Something was missing, but it might have been a few brain cells. "I've been looking for you."

"Didn't look like you were looking for a person. Looked like you were burglarizing an apartment."

"Your friend, Dani, was worried and asked me to look into your disappearance." He must look pretty suspicious. And he needed this girl's trust. "I'm Jay Hunter. I do some of the crime scene investigations for Dallas PD that you and your team clean up." Her silence spurred on more explanation. "We've talked before. Remember,

Tyrone's friend?"

"So, you decided you needed to break in and start going through… things?" Her accent vanished for an instant. Her tone lowered to a more familiar tone.

"Dani?"

"What were you looking for at the desk in the bedroom?" The high pitch returned.

The desk and bedroom instead of my desk and bedroom. "Dani, let me loose."

"Answer my question." She flashed a light in his face.

He looked down, avoiding the glare and caught sight of his hands. "Is this Scotch tape? Really?" Layers and layers of the narrow plastic mummified his hands from wrist to thumbs, though his fingers could wiggle. His knees were also attached to each other.

"It was all I could… all I had." She discarded her accent finally.

"I'll be out of this in minutes. You have to know that." He bit at one end of the plastic and pulled away a long strand.

"You stop pulling on that now, or I'll call 911. I swear. I'll leave you right here all trussed up for them to find you trying to talk your way out of breaking and entering. Bet that'll go over well with the other cops."

He paused, contemplating the death of his career. At least he'd detached enough tape to get his hands open, though still together at the wrist. "I have a warrant." Enough to give him a right to be here, but not enough to explain his current ridiculous state.

"Oh, really."

"Yes. And I'll be happy to show it to you if you get all this tape off of me."

"Where is it?"

Wow. She really had no trust in him whatsoever. What had he ever done to her except try to help? His face heated. "Somewhere you aren't going to get to."

"We'll see about that." She advanced.

She must not have noticed his partly freed hands. He grabbed hers and pulled her down. She rolled, and the inertia tumbled him onto her. With his knees locked together, he could hardly adjust to her countermove. Planting a foot in his gut, she hoisted him over her head. He landed with a thud. Great. Now his tail hurt as much as his skull. And the noise had to have alerted the people downstairs.

A dog started barking.

Dani rolled him over before he had the chance to react. She searched his back pockets as he struggled to his knees and spun around to face her.

"This is ridiculous. You asked for my help, and I'm trying to give it to you. Now let me loose." Though the activity had gone a long way to releasing his knees.

"Not while I still have my doubts." She reached for her dropped flashlight and examined the warrant in its beam while he pulled off the tape from his wrists. With them undone, he broke through the few layers attaching his knees together.

"All properly signed, or do you think I'm a forger as well as a cat burglar?" He jerked the slip from her hand and shoved it back into his pocket. "You promised you would back off and let me handle this."

She handed him his flashlight. Probably picked it up in the other room where she clobbered him. "Only if you would handle it."

"What's that supposed to mean? I'm obviously investigating, or I wouldn't be here."

"Hmm." Her flashlight scanned the room to the front door. "Well, if that's the case, we'd better get out of here."

His neck stiffened. "Tell me you didn't call the police."

"I didn't, but I bet the folks below us did. Tasha always had complaints from them."

He jerked open the front door and headed for the lot.

She caught his arm and pulled him back. "Not that way. The neighbors will be watching." She jogged silently to the opposite stairs and down to a sidewalk which seemed to circle the entire complex. At least she believed in him enough to lead him in the right direction.

They hiked the perimeter of the complex. The lot seemed quiet as normal when they reached Dani's car.

"Where's yours?" She unlocked her door.

"Down the block a bit. I didn't want to advertise a police presence even though it's unmarked."

"Get in."

He folded himself into the Honda. Smaller, but much cleaner than his. The interior practically shined.

"Did you find anything?" She did a turn around the lot toward the exit.

"Thought I had. Receipts and papers caught in the back of her desk drawer, but none of it seemed important."

"Just missed by whoever searched the place."

"And you're right about the search. Thorough job."

She circled the block and paused at Jay's car about the time a silent cruiser entered the apartment lot, lights whirling.

Jay rubbed his hands together, flaking off excess adhesive. "Well, you can be sure your friend's disappearance will be investigated now."

"Yeah…." Her lip curled downward.

"I thought you'd be happy." He fished in his pocket for his keychain.

"I'm glad, all right, but I just remembered that I left my crowbar on Tasha's porch."

Not likely to be missed. So much for escaping implication.

Chapter Five

The next morning after her Bible study, Dani shrugged on her heavy coat and hiked to the bank of mailboxes that serviced her side of the complex. The wind had died sometime during the night leaving a crystal sky of robin's egg blue without a cloud or a smidgeon of haze. The weather itself seemed to want to encourage her. Something good would happen today. She knew it.

She shoved her key into the lock. Usually grabbing the mail was an afterwork ritual, but the events of the day before had distracted her, and she'd forgotten to come.

Who was she kidding? The man that got a warrant to investigate Tasha's apartment is what distracted her. Or rather, who. All night, she'd wrestled with troubling thoughts—either worries over Tasha or concern over what Jay thought of her. Poor guy. She needed to take him some pain medication.

She collected a handful of flyers and bills and reached for a padded envelope in the back of the box. What was that? She hadn't ordered anything. She dared not. Having her name on the apartment lease and the requirements that went along with renting were about the extent of her record here.

The return address was from Iowa. A PO Box. The town was smeared, but the name started with an R. Maybe a K? Did she know anyone in Iowa?

Not as Dani Foster, but that was the name on the package. She carried the mail back to her apartment. Stacking the rest from biggest to smallest on the corner of her coffee table, she took the package into her room and opened the drapes that covered her patio door. With full light and a nice view of the field behind her home, she pulled at the flap of the envelope until she opened one edge.

Inside was a plastic bag containing a ring. Looked familiar. Brownish stones. No wait, chocolate diamonds. She'd seen some for the first time a few weeks ago at a cleaning job. That ring she'd discovered under the veneer of the dresser.

This ring. Or at least it looked like the same one. A row of small white stones entwined with a row of darker ones. Then a large chocolate diamond rose above the others, on a pedestal. She checked the inside of the band. Same engraving.

It looked valuable. But how had it come into her possession? This didn't make sense. She peered into the envelope again. A crumpled sheet of notebook paper hid at the bottom. She tugged it out, spread it on the table, and glanced at the signature.

Tasha.

Her hands shook as she held the letter in the sunlight streaming through the glass door. Her friend's usual tight manuscript looked more like chicken scratch. She must have been terrified.

Dear Dani,

Someone's following me. I don't have time to write it all out, but I'm mailing this ring to you for safe keeping. Not sure how it came to be at Pete's Pawn last week. I'm meeting with Jay Hunter about the situation this afternoon. Hopefully I'll get some answers.

She'd spoken to Jay? Why hadn't he

mentioned that? Ugly thoughts filled Dani's head. How Jay had made her promise to leave the investigating to him. How he had failed to turn over the photos to Kirkland and secretly broke into Tasha's place. Even if he did have a warrant. She wished she'd gotten a better look at that paper.

Could he have something to do with Tasha's disappearance?

Her phone sounded with Tyrone's ringtone. She picked up the call. "Heard from Tasha?"

"I was hoping you had. But I still think she's all right."

Funny, the shake in the man's voice claimed the opposite. Why hadn't she told him about what she'd seen? Well, at least she could explain that the investigation was going on. "I turned in a missing person's report on her. I bet the cops are in on it now."

"They'll figure things out then." His tone widened. It always did when he smiled, and the man was a perpetual smiler. "But I wanted to remind you about tonight."

Ugh. The birthday dinner. "Oh, but Ty—"

"Don't even start with me. You promised. What else do you have to do anyway?" He chuckled.

"Poke around at a pawn shop." Shoot, had she said that out loud?

"What pawn shop?" He blew a puff into the phone. "You sound like Tasha."

"I think she might have gone to a place called Pete's Pawn last weekend. I'm just going to drop by on my way to the warehouse." Even to her, the explanation sounded weak. Besides, it didn't conflict with the birthday dinner, so she couldn't use it to excuse herself from that.

"Take care, little girl. If the cops are investigating like you say, you should let them do their jobs and stay out of their way."

"Oh, I won't get in their way. A little curious. That's all."

"Uh-huh. You know where that leads. Whatever it is, just make sure you plan to meet us tonight. Carla will be disappointed if you don't show."

Guilt trip. She shut her eyes. "I'll be there." She glanced at the clock. Not much time before she was due at the job site. "I'll talk to you more in a bit."

She folded the envelope into the zippered section of her shoulder bag and returned her phone to the side pocket. Shrugging on her winter coat, she exited and sprinted down the outside stairs. The dash to her car exhilarated her, but by the time she reached the Honda at the edge of her lot, she was chilled. She ducked onto her seat, turned on the engine, and cranked up the heater. She rubbed her hands together before shifting to weave her way out of the lot.

At a light, she looked up Pete's Pawn on her phone. It backed up to the street address for Tasha's complex. She probably stopped by there all the time.

Dani drove by Tasha's place on her way to the shop. She turned in to the virtually empty lot and backed into a spot where she had a good view of the landing. She blew out a long exhale as she gazed at the yellow police tape that crossed Tasha's door. Finally. Maybe Tyrone was right about letting the experts handle Tasha's disappearance. Should she turn over the ring and letter she'd received?

If she was right, this ring had already been in police possession a few weeks ago, yet somehow it wound up in a pawn shop. How could she turn it over to anyone there until she knew who could be trusted? And that even included Jay Hunter. Especially included him, since he might have been the last person to talk to Tasha before she disappeared. And he had neglected to mention that important detail.

Leaving her car in the lot, she rounded the block. Dirty, empty storefronts stared at her, like the blank windows of a ghost town. Far from the freeway and connecting routes, the area was almost barren. The shop was the third address down, but the first actual business she came to.

She pushed through the door and eyed the store's interior. Ew. Dust danced in the beams of light wafting through the windows. Walls closed in with overstuffed shelves and glass cases filling every open space. She sneezed into her elbow and wiped the tip of her nose with her finger.

"What can I do you for?" A fifty-ish fellow with a scruffy face and a receding hairline stood behind the cluttered counter. A small TV in the corner carried strains from a familiar daytime drama.

She tugged the ring out of the envelope in her purse. "I was wondering about this." She carried it to him and pinched her fingers over the closure of the plastic bag. "Please don't touch it."

"You're no cop." He tucked his chin and multiplied it.

Was it such a reach to believe she could be a detective like her father? "No. I received this from a friend. She bought it here, but I...." Choose your words carefully. "... uh... it looks valuable. Maybe even old."

"Don't look old to me." He fingered the baggie. A bar code sticker was on one side of it. He pulled up a piece of register tape and copied down the numbers. "Say she bought it here?"

"That's what she told me."

He stood and eyed her from her sneakers up. His smolder made her mouth sour. She pursed her lips together to keep her disgust from painting her face.

"Got a receipt?" The man reached for the baggie, but she shoved it back into her purse.

He shrugged then buried his fingers in a card file.

Innocent question on the surface. Her dad had explained all sort of cons. This one was popular with shady shop owners—claiming something the customer owned was actually lifted from their store. Shop owner's word against the customer's unless there was a receipt involved.

Dani cocked her eyebrow. If he wanted to treat her like some naïve child, let him. "My friend has it. Would you like for me to call her?" A bluff, not a lie. Tasha probably did have a receipt somewhere in the clutter of the apartment. Unless someone had found it already. Maybe it was in that stack that Jay had mentioned.

"Hmph." He shut the lid of the card file. "Wait here. I think this is in a file in the back room." He waddled through a curtain in the back.

Dani's nose tickled. Didn't anyone ever dust this place? She wandered, browsing, toward one of the shelves. A lone China cup sat next to a Palm Pilot from the 90s and a scarred Brownie camera. She picked up the cup and turned it over. Royal Doulton. "Where's your family, little guy?" She put it back on the shelf and shifted the Palm Pilot to a stack of electronics on lower level. A table on her left held a marble chess set. She began to arrange the pieces for the beginning of a game but found several missing. Were they lost before the set arrived, or did they walk away after it got here?

A place like this surely made Tasha drool. Porcelain dolls, miniature marble figurines, coins, paintings. The musty smell left Dani wheezing. She coughed and dug in her bag for a tissue. That clerk sure was taking a long time. "Did you find anything?"

Silence.

Closing the gap between the main counter and the curtain meant weaving around several overflowing tables and a couple of bins spilling their contents onto the floor. She didn't like wasting time, and patience had never been a strong suit.

But the man was obviously in no hurry. She might as well chill.

The murmur of voices from the TV grew. An argument of some sort. She strolled around the corner of the counter to get a better view. Some buxom blonde was chewing out a shirtless man. A weightlifter by the looks of his glistening shoulders. The argument didn't amount to much. A few tangled sentences, some sultry glances full of accusation and pouty lips, then a final comment from the woman that caused the man to completely change his attitude.

How many times had she and her high school friends turned on one of these dramas without the sound so they could make their own dialogue? Usually in Dani's living room with a bowl of popcorn to pass around. And Dad would join them with a quip here and there, causing an eruption of giggles.

Her dad would've already found Tasha. But he'd be mad as anything about Dani putting herself in such dangerous situations.

She rounded the counter again and called out a little louder. "Hey, Mister, are you still back there?" Why didn't he answer? The silence mocked Dani's stupidity.

She could almost hear her father chewing her out. *You need to engage those wonderful gray cells that God gave you before you act stupid.* And she was acting stupid now. Standing there waiting for what? That man could stomp right in here with a gun. There were plenty of those hanging on the walls. What stopped him from chloroforming Dani and landing her in the same sauce as Tasha?

Shouldering her purse, she made for the door just as he came through the curtain. "Sorry, that piece was an anonymous sale, I guess. Maybe part of some estate collection or something, but I don't know anything about it."

That was strange. She tensed. What had he been doing back there? She scanned him. No weapon in front. He turned to pull the fabric closed revealing a lower than needed waistband. An ugly sight, but at least it proved he was unarmed. Good. She blew out her exhale. "You've only had it for a short time, right?" A few weeks at the most.

"Couldn't say." He sat and turned the TV volume higher.

A commercial about feminine hygiene seemed to capture his attention. His hand shook as he reached for his coffee cup. Covering for someone? This man had discarded the arrogant attitude he'd had when he went through the curtain. What was back there? Or who?

"Can I borrow your bathroom?"

"Employees only." He didn't look at her.

Boy, did he ever want her to leave. She could practically hear the bass tones shouting, "Get out" in a ghostly echo.

"I thought I might find a necklace or some earrings that matched this ring." That sounded like a logical reason for her to be here and ask about the origin of the piece.

"I'm busy." He shifted his gaze and stared her down.

Funny how his words seemed to have that same creepy echo in her head. She turned and ambled through the entrance. Fat lotta good that trip did her. Turning left, she backtracked along the sketchy street. A few cars were parked along the sidewalk. No telling where their owners were. With all the potholes in the pavement, no wonder few cars traveled this route.

She passed a broken-down Plymouth when something whizzed by her ear. Instinct kicked in and she ducked. Someone stood across the street, partly hidden behind the remains of an empty gas station. She squatted and put her back to the circa 1980s vehicle. Thick glass in the storefront behind her thunked but didn't shatter. The window had a number of bullet holes.

A bullet? Someone shot at her? The passenger seat window above her shattered and rained down like shimmering hail stones.

Snatching her phone from her purse, she dialed 9-1-1 and gave the dispatcher her location as she moved toward the front of the car. She peered over the hood, through the windshield in search of the person she'd seen. A man she thought but didn't see another glimpse of him.

The metal on the mirror across from her pinged, and she ducked again. Wherever the guy was, he had a bead on her. She eyed the entrance to the pawn shop. No guessing what the clerk had been doing in the backroom, now.

But his store seemed her only option. If she

could make it there.

A truck rumbled in her direction. She peered around the backside of the Plymouth. An old flatbed toting a totaled sedan. The vehicle moved at a lumbering speed but slowed more for the deep breaks in the asphalt.

Dani used the opportunity. With the truck blocking the view of the gas station, she darted back to the pawn shop and bolted through the front door. The creepy guy no longer sat behind the counter, but the TV still blared. Without hesitating, she split the curtains and slowed for a moment as she maneuvered through the back room toward a door at the opposite end.

"Hey." Creepy dude was hunkered into near fetal position by the inside wall. "You're not supposed to be back here." He pointed at her.

"No, I'm supposed to be getting shot out front." She glared at him. "Sorry for the inconvenience." Hopefully he didn't miss the accusation in her tone.

She busted through the exit and caught the view of her car still across the alley in Tasha's lot. Her speed propelled her in that direction. With God's blessings, she'd made it this far. That truck had been heaven-sent. Of that she was sure. And she wasn't about to doubt His protection, now.

Jay squeezed the bridge of his nose, willing the throb in his head to go away. At least the bump was under his hair. How would he have explained such a bruise?

He eyed the information on his computer screen. Natasha Sanderson had grown up in Camden, Iowa and lived there, attending school, until her mother died about four months ago. Then, she'd moved to Dallas. According to Dani, to be closer to her aunt. She enrolled in law school. Nothing beyond that. Not even a ticket.

He'd followed up with the aunt, talking to one of the workers at the center in which she lived. Dani was right. There had been no visitors.

Dead end.

Then he typed in the name Danielle Foster.

What he thought would be a simple process turned into an all-morning struggle. He found evidence of her arrival in the metroplex, hard to say when exactly. But no trace before that. Even a maiden name would've shown up somewhere. Either he was losing his touch, or she drastically changed her identity.

Why would she do that?

Scowling, he eyed his phone as it drummed out a Latin beat. Tyrone again. He had half a mind to punch the hang-up button, but maybe he had news about Tasha or Dani.

"What gruesome scene are you working today?" He mustered his last ounce of good humor and threw it into the conversation. How long before he could take another acetaminophen?

"Nothing yet. Besides, you're the one who always gets there first. But when we do get done today, Carla and I are entertaining tonight and thought you could finally join us." Tyrone's tone always sounded cheery. Without even trying most of the time. Why couldn't Jay have joy like that?

"Not really up to a party tonight."

Tyrone and his wife had thrown every female specimen they found at him, hoping one of them would make a connection. Like flinging dry spaghetti at a wall.

Jay had been down that road and had no intention of revisiting.

"No party, just dinner at El Suarez. Your favorite spot."

Uh oh. All-out matchmaking was much worse

than a party. "I got a… a thing."

"A thing?" Judging from Ty's voice, he had no intention of letting him off the hook.

"Yeah. I need… uh…." He picked up a pencil and twirled it between his fingers like he had when he was a drummer in high school.

"Don't mess with me, Jay. This is Carla's birthday. And you promised last time that you would go with us to the next night out."

A couple of weeks ago when they wanted to hook him up with a Cowboy cheerleader, he'd declined and promised for the next time. He got the feeling at this point that the cheerleader wasn't the true set-up.

He tapped out a beat on the desk mat. "All right. All right. For Carla's birthday." If nothing else, he'd enjoy a few laughs with Tyrone and some fine Tex-Mex. If he could dispel this headache. "I'll meet you there, I guess."

"About seven."

"That late? Won't y'all be done with your job before then?"

"We haven't even started yet."

An afternoon job? No wonder dinner would be so late. "Is Dani with you?" He wouldn't share about the night before but wondered how the woman fared this morning. Better than he had, he suspected.

"Dani?" He could hear the smile through the connection. "Something going on between you two?"

Sigh. "No, I've been looking into Tasha's disappearance. Dani will likely hear from her before anyone else, right?"

"Yeah. She's meeting me on site, today. Said she had a lead at some pawn shop called Pete's."

"What are you talking about?"

"Tasha called herself a treasure hunter. Dani thought she went to Pete's this weekend."

Jay's stomach contracted. A buzz had gone around the station about a daytime shooting at a pawn shop. Saying goodbye to his friend, he snatched up his keys and he headed for the door.

Dani had to stop sticking her nose into Tasha's disappearance.

Chapter Six

Dani turned north onto Preston Road. Stopping at a light, she cranked up her heater and pasted her phone to her ear. What was Matthew Donaldson doing? She makes an emergency call to her security contact, and he puts her on hold? What kind of witness-security agent does that?

"You still there, Dani?"

"You better hope so, or your case goes out the window. By now, Demitriadis could have slit my throat or kidnapped me or—"

"Repainted your fence?"

"What?" For a member of such an exalted secret agency, Matt often made little sense. His sponge-like personality sucked the joy right out of the air.

"That's what he's doing now. Repainting a fence at the city jail. Community service."

"Then he sent someone for me." She eyed the red light. Way too slow. Her gaze hit her mirror. Had that white panel van been behind her when she fled from the lot at Tasha's apartment?

"Try not to let your imagination run away, Dani. Demitriadis is under wraps. Or don't you think we know how to do our jobs?"

She didn't but angering her witness security contact didn't bode well. "I didn't say that, Matt, but someone shot at me."

"Backfire."

Grr. He was impossible. "I'm a cop's daughter. You don't think I know the difference?"

"You didn't the last time you called me in such a panic."

She'd never live that down. "That was... unusual." Terrified, her emotions had blocked out logical thought. "I'm not irrational now."

"You sound irrational to me." He droned on about the cases he worked, the support he offered, and how she alone stole more time from him than any of his other clients.

Only half-listening, she transferred the phone to speaker and snapped it into its holder as she weighed her options. Going home was impossible. She could take off on her own, but without help, money, or a place to go, she'd come whimpering back to Matt in no time. The fact was she needed the minimal support and protection connections that he and his agency provided.

And according to the agency, Demitriadis still had no idea where, or who, she was. Better yet, neither did his boss.

She tried to release her anxiety in an exhale, but it didn't work. "I hear what you're saying, Matt. And I'm sorry that my calls are tiresome. Someone wants me dead. I live with that knowledge every stinking day. And now, out on the street in broad daylight, someone is shooting at me. And no, it wasn't a backfire, because he was using a silencer. He got close enough to leave a bullet hole in a plate glass window and shatter the car pane right over my head. If you don't want to be concerned about that, then I guess I'm better off on my own."

"Don't go rogue on me, Dani."

"Apparently, you have one too many clients. And since I'm the one who's causing most of the trouble, I should be the one to go."

"I didn't mean it like that. I simply believe

you're being paranoid."

Oh, this man. "I'll think about that as I consider my options. Thank you for your time." She hit the end button.

Her? Paranoid? Who had time to imagine danger with people obviously trying to kill her?

Why didn't the light change? The people around her appeared just as irritated as she felt.

Except the man kneeling near the electrical box on the corner. He looked up, directly at her. Beady black eyes beneath a shaved receding hairline. He smiled and glanced at his toolbox.

Did he have a gun in there? Had he paused the traffic meter in order to delay her so he could complete his assassination? She stiffened and scanned the cross street. Trapped by traffic. Was this the ploy that would finish the job for Dimitriadis? A lull approached.

She cut her eyes again to the man who was pulling tools from his box with rapid determination. He seemed to settle on a screwdriver. But Dani didn't want to wait around until he found something else. She sped into the intersection receiving beeps and gestures.

Weaving around someone turning left, she shot across the gap and escaped to the other side.

She made a quick right onto an empty, wide road and accelerated, her eyes as much on her rear view as focused in front. She hadn't imagined the gunshots, no matter what Matt believed. And that grimy guy working at Pete's had set her up.

A quick check showed that no one followed. She slowed and released the breath she held. *Thank you for your protection, Lord. At least, You're always there for me. Even if my security contact thinks I'm not worth the effort. You do.*

Taking a left, she wove through back streets to the job site where she would meet Tyrone. After all, where else could she go at this point?

Hopefully she'd never truly have to depend on her Wit-Sec agent. She'd never survive.

At least she knew where she stood with the man. Not like that crime scene specialist who pretended to help her. She thought back to her conversations with Jay. What had sounded like concern had really been a cover-up. He'd met with Tasha. Maybe even arranged for her to disappear.

The fact that he hadn't said anything about their meeting or mentioned her phone call confirmed his duplicity. But she'd have to find some way besides using Pete's Pawn to give credence to her suspicions.

She found the job site. Yellow police tape marked the porch of the frame house. She parked far to the right of the property where she wouldn't be in the way of the truck when Tyrone arrived.

She called the non-emergency number for Jay's department. The receptionist transferred her to the crime scene unit.

"This is Cutter."

Dani didn't recognize the name, but the voice sounded familiar. "I'm looking for Jay Hunter. Is he available?"

"Sorry, he's not in. Do you want to leave a message?"

"My name is Dani Foster." Oh. Why did she give her name? "Not really. I, well… do you know where he is?"

"He said something about visiting a pawn shop, Ms. Foster. Would you like me to have him call you?"

She startled. He'd gone to a pawn shop? "No. No. I…." Had he been the man shooting at her? "Forget I called. Thanks."

Her mind whirled to the brief image of the man she'd seen. Hard to say. She hadn't been able to tell much with a shapeless hoodie covering his head and torso. It could have been Jay.

Why would he shoot at her?

Her phone chimed with the generic ringtone, and she glanced at the screen. Jay? Calling her? No way would she take that. Not now. She hit the end button and switched her phone off.

Not until she figured out whose side he was really on.

Jay glanced up at the neon El Suarez sign that loomed over the restaurant parking lot. If only the foggy beacon could illuminate what was going on with Dani. The day had led to frustration and more questions.

He'd set out immediately for Pete's Pawn but found several police cars surrounding the place. The only word he could get was that there'd been shots fired. No report of injury, thank the Lord.

Circling the block had offered no sign of Dani's car and, of course, she wouldn't answer her cell. He'd even headed out to Kellerman's but found it empty except for a receptionist. She offered him plenty of unwanted female attention, but no help.

Even Tyrone had proved a dead end most of

the day. He'd called him at least four times, but he didn't answer any better than Dani.

They had probably been on the site and up to their knees in the remains of human chaos.

Finally, Jay gave up and turned his attention to the tasks he actually got paid to do. But as the evening neared, dread grew. If only he'd stood his ground about attending this evening's masqueraded blind date. Who might it be this time? Carla's hairdresser? No, he'd already met her. What about Tyrone's dental hygienist? Wait, he'd met her, too. And they couldn't set him up with any of the women at their church. No way any of them would do that again.

At least his headache had dissipated.

He stared up at the sign marking the restaurant that had been his favorite since childhood. Today, the yellow and green lights didn't enchant him. He wasn't in the mood for a girl to be flung his direction even if it was Carla's birthday. He ground his molars and pulled the gift bag out of his passenger seat.

A narrow alley separated the restaurant from its wide parking lot, and he jogged across. One of the mainstays of downtown Dallas, the building looked better suited for a quaint, suburban intersection than for the chrome and glass that surrounded it. The never-ending hum from the freeway reminded him of the things he needed to sort out.

And just because Dani stopped investigating long enough to work didn't mean she'd leave the issue alone this evening. The thought twisted in his chest.

He climbed the steps to the porch and glanced toward the famous West End Marketplace—the little that he could see of the warehouse district-turned night spot under the freeway bridge that separated them. Cars filled every open spot of pavement, and beyond, colored lights shown from tiny windows between the original brick of the historic buildings. Crowds of people milled around, likely visiting the many bars and restaurants.

Why couldn't he be like that? Carefree. Having fun without stewing over things that had happened or worrying about what might occur.

Jay pulled out his phone. Maybe now that Dani wasn't at work, she'd answer. He dialed and listened until her message came on. His brow furrowed as he pocketed the phone. This would be a short dinner. Then, he'd drive by Dani's place and make sure she wasn't doing anymore wall-climbing. He pulled on the twisted iron bar attached to the extra-large wooden door.

Several couples and families waited to be seated. El Suarez was busy at mid-week, but he wasn't surprised. Surrounded by familiarity, he tried to let the feel of the formal Spanish villa envelope him. He glanced at the wall-sized portrait of a bullfighter poised for a kill. The subject matter did little to comfort him. In fact, he could see himself as the bull about to be skewered.

He gave his information to the host, who led him toward the main dining room. Colorful paintings of dancing señoritas decorated each wall with a huge town scene depicting old Mexico on the broadest space. Tyrone and Carla sat under a collection of colorful piñatas near the mural and were talking to someone across the table.

He recognized Dani's partial profile, the tilt of her chin and her cheek peeking from behind a cascade of brown hair. A weight lifted. She wasn't investigating, scaling rooftops. She was… his date for the evening? Hmm. Interesting.

Tyrone caught his eye and rose to shake his hand. Dani turned a smiling face in his direction. Then their eyes met and her smile evaporated.

Chapter Seven

Agh. What was he doing here?

Dani shut her mouth against the initial shock and turned her back on Jay as he greeted Tyrone.

Of all the restaurants in Dallas, they had to choose the particular one that Jay would visit on he same night. Despite her heavy sweater, a chill frosted her back.

Jay leaned toward Carla, gave her a half hug, and handed her a bright yellow gift bag. He knew it was her birthday?

Before she had the chance to contemplate his action further, he took the seat next to her. "Nice to see you tonight, Dani."

His arm brushed hers, leaving a tingling sensation over the ice that had thickened around her. She mumbled something of a hello.

"Are you surprised?" Tyrone beamed. If he knew Jay was in on Tasha's disappearance, he wouldn't be so chummy.

"Shocked." Jay laughed then glanced at her. "But in a good way."

She stuck her nose in the menu and clamped her teeth shut. She would not speak without thinking tonight. No matter what.

"Any sign of your friend?" If Jay was talking to her, she wasn't going to answer.

"Still no word from her, but thanks for asking." Tyrone gave Jay far too much kindness.

Carla put down her menu. "I'm so worried about her."

Dani pulled the menu down and tried to be cordial. For Carla's sake. She didn't need to spend her birthday dinner stressed about Tasha. "I assume someone from the police department is looking into her disappearance, now."

"Yes. I saw a *Be On the Lookout* report for her just this morning. I bet we'll hear something soon." Jay dipped a chip in hot sauce. "I did speak to her aunt's nursing home again. They still haven't seen or heard from Tasha. Do you know any of her aunt's neighbors?"

Tasha had mentioned one. The lady next door to Dodie's home. What was her name?

Tyrone sipped his water. "I remember she said something about her last relative. Nothing about the neighbors, though."

Carla eyed Dani. "Do you think she might have gone back to Iowa for some reason?"

Dani shrugged, the return address on that package haunted her. "I don't know what to think. But what's good here?" She opened her menu again, hoping the change in topic stuck. It worked, but only until the waiter came for their order. Then the other three went back to surmising what might have happened to Tasha.

A big part of her wanted to jam her fists on her hips and demand that Jay tell them. He could have been the last one to see her alive. Wait. She was going way overboard. No more letting her imagination run wild.

Grabbing a chip, she sank it into the little pot of dark brown sauce.

"You might want to be careful." Jay pointed at the bowl.

"I've been in Dallas for months. You don't think I've tried hot sauce yet?"

"Yes, but that's …"

She smirked and chomped on the chip.

"… Habanero sauce."

Flame filled her mouth and seared down her throat before she wrapped her mind around what he said. "Oh." She inhaled, pulling cooled air into her mouth. Snatching her napkin, she coughed and spit the chip into the red material. "Ow." She wiped her tongue, but the heat seemed to expand.

"Here." Jay handed her his napkin.

She gulped her water but only succeeded in spreading pain.

"Oh, honey, no." Carla rounded the table and handed her a tortilla. "This will take the edge off."

Dani stuffed half of it into her mouth. Not the immediate relief she'd hoped for, but the burn stopped spreading.

Jay signaled to a waiter. "Can we get some milk and more napkins over here?"

How humiliating. Dani swallowed and wiped her tongue once more. "Oh, that was awful." She glanced to her right at a family gawking at her. Another table somewhere behind her hissed with snickers.

"Sorry I didn't stop you in time." He put his hand over his mouth. Was he chuckling through all of this? "I've been in your shoes.

Unfortunately."

"My fault." Dani's cheeks heated as much as her mouth had. The burn still ached down her throat. She swallowed several sips of milk. Between the tortilla and the milk, the searing heat subsided.

Tyrone chuckled. "At least you can say you've tried the sauce. That's better than about half the people in this city."

She coughed. "There's that."

"And you know what a dragon feels like." Jay smirked.

"Can't argue there." She chomped the final bite of tortilla.

Tyrone handed her another. "Don't sweat it. Jay teases, but you shoulda seen him with his first taste of the spicy."

"Aw, man. You don't have to bore her with details." Jay leaned back in his chair and looked at the ceiling.

"He was one of the judges for the church's salsa-making contest. Big thing last summer when Rosewood Baptist sponsored a neighborhood picnic. Anyway, Jay thought, being a native Texan and all, he was the perfect choice to judge these citified salsa cooks."

"I never said I was perfect. But I grew up in East Texas. I know what the stuff is supposed to taste like."

"Ha." Tyrone snorted. "So, the other two judges are dipping coffee stirrers into the bowls to try them out, see? But Jay thinks there's no way they can taste anything with such a tiny sample."

"Sounds reasonable." Dani enjoyed how the slight blush to Jay's face made his rugged features soften. She wiped the table in front of her with a clean napkin.

"Well, how could they get a real taste with a coffee stirrer?"

"Only they weren't tasting. Not yet. They were testing the heat. Jay blows that part off and dips a big chip into the first bowl." Tyrone guffawed.

"Dip's not dip until it stands on a chip." Jay folded his arms with a smirk.

"Yeah, well, this dip just about blew his head off. I don't know what they put in that thing, but he turned so red he coulda been an Independence Day decoration.

"It wasn't that bad." He shook his head. "But the point is I got blasted when I was trying the stuff on purpose. At least you were unintentionally burned."

"You boys are crazy." Carla buttered a flour tortilla. "I keep telling Tyrone that he has no taste since he insists on burning all his taste buds off with that lava."

"Yeah, honey, but then your idea of hot sauce comes with a blue lid."

"Blue? I've seen the green mild jars...." Jay crunched another chip.

"Nope. Carla buys the blue lid picante sauce. It's more like chunky ketchup." Tyrone laughed.

Carla put her hands on her hips. "You better not be dissing my secret ingredients. Not if you want me to treat you to chicken enchilada soup this week."

Tyrone ducked his head. "Oops. You have my deepest apologies." He raised his hand. "Her chicken enchilada soup is the best."

"You should come over, Jay. Friday night." Carla grinned from him to Dani. "And you too, sweet girl. I promise, no fire sauce on my table."

"I'm there. Love Mexican food." Jay started in on a story of a visit to Mexico last year. A mission trip to help construct a new wing at an orphanage. "The food was amazing."

A mission trip? Helping orphans? Conflicting

thoughts spun in Dani's head as Jay and Tyrone discussed mutual experiences. He was the perfect date. Kind. Funny. Gorgeous. But he might be a cold-blooded killer. How could she even relax with him? And yet, it seemed she'd agreed to be paired with him on yet another date to come.

A little tingle zipped through her at how he agreed to the dinner without hesitation. He seemed so friendly. So kind. Laughing with him and the Reids almost felt normal again.

As the night wound down, she shrugged on her coat. Tyrone had insisted on bringing her with them. Safer that way. She had to agree considering all that had happened to her during the day.

But when she anticipated catching another ride with the couple, Jay offered to transport her.

Dani stiffened. Did she trust Jay enough to be alone with him? To let him take her all the way to her home? He still hadn't mentioned meeting with Tasha or even her friend's phone call.

Tyrone laid his arm around his wife's shoulders. "That would really help us out. We have another stop to make on the way home tonight."

She couldn't really argue with them. Not without embarrassing herself. Why hadn't she insisted in bringing her own car?

The safety issue that Tyrone talked about went out the window if Jay really did have something to do with Tasha's disappearance. After spending the evening with him, though, she had trouble believing that. With her hopes and guard high, she said good night to her friends and let him escort her to the door.

Three different women smiled at him in that short distance. Dani lifted her shoulders and glanced his way. He didn't seem to notice the appreciation. His dark eyes steady on the exit, his cropped dark hair over his smooth tanned face. Exotic. Yeah, she was being ushered out by the hottest man in the building. She squashed thoughts of what else he might be.

When he put his hand to her back she flinched. It was just his hand. She curled hers into balls in the bottoms of her coat pockets and maintained a pleasant expression.

He led her across the one-lane street. "Had you been here before?"

"No. I mean, I've had Tex-Mex. Can't avoid it in this town. But not here. I liked it, though."

She ducked into the passenger seat of the car. Cleaner this time than the last time she'd gotten in.

And it smelled fresh instead of like fried food. She picked at a piece of lint on the dashboard and tossed it out the door as he shut it for her.

He strolled around the car and climbed into his seat. "My favorite since I was small. But not so much the Habanero Sauce." He chuckled, lightening her mood and easing the tightening muscles across her shoulders.

Her cheeks warmed again. "I'm pretty good at making a fool of myself." She mustered a rueful laugh.

Glancing at her, he silenced for a moment. "A fool? No. Not at all." His smile lit his eyes, and the ice wall she'd been trying to rebuild dropped into a warm, mud puddle.

She was either completely wrong about this man, or he was an Emmy-worthy actor.

Quiet ensued as he wove through the city streets and merged onto the freeway. "I know you're upset about Tasha. I wish I had answers for you."

Shame engulfed her. She'd stopped thinking about her missing friend for a few moments as she enjoyed his profile and lingered on some of the evening's fun. "She would have contacted me by now. If she could."

Traffic slowed. "Looks like an accident." Jay turned on his scanner and flashing lights. He reported the tie-up location while he maneuvered around what was left of a Smart Car, a pickup, and a sedan. "Can you help with some basic first aid?" He shoved the car into park and grabbed two sets of latex gloves from the dash compartment.

She nodded and slipped on a pair. Déjà vu. Only this time, instead of being her father's helper, she assisted a man she didn't trust. Not fully anyway, even with the laughter they'd shared through dinner. She followed him to the first car. Uninhabited. A young woman sat in a fetal position on the shoulder of the road.

"Check on her."

Dani didn't need the order. She knelt in front of the girl, ignoring the rocks that dug into her bare knees. Her own stupidity for wearing a dress on such a cold night. "Are you injured?"

The girl looked up. Streaks of mascara painted her face. "I think." She held out her hands where they had been crossed over her legs. Both knees of her bleach-streaked blue jeans were covered in blood. Was that from her hands or the other way around?

Dani examined one of her hands and found no

trace of injury. Without knowing the source of the blood, she opted to have the girl stay as she was. "Do your knees hurt?"

"I don't know what happened."

Dani took off her coat and wrapped it around the girl's shoulders.

Sirens wailed. A few other drivers had stopped to assist. One woman approached. "I'm a nurse. Can I help you?"

"She has blood on her knees, but I can't tell what's bleeding."

The woman nodded and set down a case resembling Jay's. "I'll take care of you, sugar."

A man, the nurse's husband maybe, came alongside her, going through the items in the box with practiced ease.

Dani scanned the area. An ambulance was having trouble weaving through the traffic. A couple of men were helping the driver of the pickup out of his cab. Jay and some others were working on a person lying on the concrete outside the sedan. A woman sobbed next to him.

She hurried toward the woman and urged her back several feet. "My name's Dani. Do you know your name?"

"That's my husband."

"Can you tell me his name?"

"Marv. Marvin Elliot." She heaved a breath and broke into another fit of tears, wrapping her large, warm arms around Dani's frozen shoulders.

"Let me pray for Marv, okay?" Without thought Dani burst into a discussion with God, beseeching Him to take care of Marv, to let the paramedics reach him quickly, to comfort Mrs. Elliot. She didn't know where the words came from. She didn't even like to pray aloud at a dinner table, but the Spirit took over, pouring out assurance and hope for this woman.

She stopped crying, but when Dani said "amen" and backed away, the woman had a mesmerized appearance. Her eyes stared in the direction of Marv, even when emergency workers blocked all possible view of the man. "Thank you, dear."

The woman had an eerie, detached voice. Was she going into some sort of emotional shock?

"Mrs. Elliot, how long have the two of you been married?"

"Forty-two years. Forty-three next month." Her voice began to warm. "Marv was my best friend's brother. Never thought much about him until he ventured home from college. So good-looking and strong." She sniffed. "He's such an amazing man."

The EMTs took over for Jay and the others working on Marv. He stepped closer, but Dani kept an arm around Mrs. Elliot. "That's funny. That's how my mom and dad met. But my mom was the one who came home. She'd been a nurse overseas on the mission field."

"My, my. That sounds like an adventure." The words only held a little inflection.

"She'd been in France, helping at a children's hospital."

She broke her gaze from her husband and glanced at Dani. "Marv took me to France once. To Paris and all of the wine country."

"That sounds like a heavenly trip. A second honeymoon?"

The woman's features softened. "Something like that, but we'd not had a first, so I guess it was both all wrapped up in one amazing journey." The men placed Marv on a gurney and rolled him toward the ambulance.

He was moving.

Mrs. Elliot rushed forward. Dani followed as Jay helped the older woman around the debris toward the ambulance.

When she reached the medical workers, she turned and touched Dani's face. "I'm going to be praying for you, Dani." Then she trotted to Marv's side and climbed into the back of the ambulance.

Mrs. Elliot and her husband would continue to be in Dani's prayers as well.

Jay held his hand out to Dani. His formerly white shirt had streaks and blotches of red all over it. His hair was mussed, and the knees of his gray slacks were almost white from crawling and kneeling on the filthy shoulder of the freeway.

Dani took his hand. Warm, strong, sure, and comforting. If nothing else, she knew she needed to figure out how to fully trust Jay Hunter.

Grime Beat

Chapter Eight

Jay walked her to the car. Her cream-colored dress didn't offer much protection against the wind with those elbow length sleeves. At least her clothes hadn't been damaged. Not that he could see. Shame he couldn't say the same for his own. His blood-stained shirt hugged his torso.

He opened her door and helped her in.

"Do you think Marv will be okay?"

Such a tender heart. How did she survive in that job of hers? "I think we got to him in time. I can check on him tomorrow if you want."

She smiled as he closed her door. Rounding the car, he popped open the trunk and pulled his shirt and undershirt over his head. He packed them into a ball and threw it into a corner. Then he removed a clean tee shirt from the duffel he always carried. Shame it wasn't another button-down or something with long sleeves. He climbed behind the wheel and noticed Dani shiver. "Where's your coat?" He cranked the heater.

"I left it with the girl. I think she was going into shock. What about yours?" Her eyes dipped to his torso.

His face heated. Caveman Triathlon. Clean but faded and with bleach marks. Couldn't he have done better than that?

He rubbed his neck with one hand. "Marv. Hard to get blood out of wool anyway." Shifting gears, he pulled back onto the freeway.

She pivoted in her seat. "I think I've misjudged you, Jay, but I need you to be honest with me."

What hadn't he been honest about? "O-kay?"

"What did you do with the photos?"

He scanned the traffic ahead of him as he tried to process. Photos... he hadn't noticed anything like that on Natasha's desk. "Like a scrapbook?"

"No, the pictures." She pointed to his visor. "The ones you put up there."

"Oh." He exited the freeway and stopped at a

light. "I turned them in. I told you I would." He pulled down the visor to show her the empty place where they had been stored.

She crossed her arms. "Kirkland said he never got them. How do you explain that?"

He cocked an eyebrow. "I thought you said you had misjudged me."

"You're avoiding the question."

"And you've already decided on my guilt." He was avoiding, but only because accusation highlighted her oval face.

Blowing out a heavy exhale, she unfolded her arms and laid them in her lap. "Fine. Did you happen to give the photos of Tasha to Officer Kirkland?" She painted on a tight smile and batted her eyelashes.

Hoo-boy she was cute. The light changed, turning his attention back to the road. "I did not."

"There. You admit it." She slapped her hands on her thighs.

"I admit nothing." Why was she so determined to convict him of some deception? "Kirkland isn't great with computers."

"So?"

"So I scanned the pictures into the file myself." He made a sharp right and parked in front of a strip mall. "I'll prove it to you." He touched the tablet mounted against his dashboard and searched for the missing-person information. "There." Two pictures popped up on Tasha's page. Kirkland hadn't even typed her name in correctly, but Jay had fixed it. Along with her hair color.

Dani leaned closer to the screen. Her shoulders slumped.

She looked downright disappointed that he wasn't a crook. Not so cute anymore.

He pulled open a compartment above his rear-view mirror and extracted a plastic cd holder. "I put them in here so they wouldn't get bent."

"I'm sorry." She tucked the case into the purse at her feet. "I'm sure you have an equally good reason for why you never mentioned that you spoke to Tasha last Saturday."

Was she accusing him again? No bite to her words, but why would she think he'd spent any time with her friend? "I barely know the girl." He shifted to drive and did a circle in the lot.

"She told me she met with you."

He halted the car with a jerk and glared at her. "I thought she was missing. Did she call you?" What sort of game was Dani playing?

Her eyes widened, but she straightened in her seat. "I got a note in the mail. She knew someone shadowed her but planned to meet with you and felt sure her problem would be solved." She faced his glare with equal intensity. "What did she say to you?"

"I didn't meet with your friend." He turned his attention back to the street. "And I never talked to her last weekend. Not on the phone. Not in an email. Not in person. Not once."

"Then why would she tell me she'd set up an appointment with you?" Her tone softened, and she leaned against the seat-back.

Her question burned through his chest.

Dani focused on the road illuminated by Jay's headlights. A shopping bag blew in front of the car before it hung on a branch in the median. She hugged her shoulders as much from the chill inside her as that on the outside.

Who was the liar? And why? Circles of thoughts turned into a Gordian knot. Jay had to be lying about meeting with Tasha. But he seemed so sincere. And he hadn't lied about anything else.

If she believed him, Tasha was lying about meeting with him. But why would she?

Finding an item that should be in the evidence lock-up must have shocked her. Of course, she'd speak to one of the crime scene guys about it. And Jay or his partner were the logical choice since they'd been the team working the suicide.

But Tasha never made an appointment with Jay. Not according to him. Was he covering something up? Or had she deliberately misled Dani?

Dani put her hands over her face as Jay pulled the car into her lot.

"You all right?"

She wiped her cheeks and forehead. "I suppose. I don't get this, though."

"What did Tasha tell you? Exactly?"

Relaying the message came easily enough, but the words comprised only part of it. Should she share about the ring? Show it to him? She pulled her purse into her lap and relayed what she could remember of the letter.

He studied the steering wheel until she finished speaking. "So she found something and wanted to talk to me about it? Why me?"

Dani sighed, fingered the plastic baggie in the

inside pocket of the leather satchel, and took another breath. "Because of this." She held the baggie toward him.

In the darkness of the lot, the item barely showed. Jay took it from her and used his penlight to examine the ring. "What is this?"

"You've never seen it?"

He shook his head.

"It's part of the evidence we discovered at the suicide a couple of weeks ago."

He froze, staring at her for an instant, then squinted. "The evidence I missed? You're sure?"

"Positive. It has an engraving on the band, 'Dear Dahlia.'" She rotated the bag in his hand. His warmth enveloped her fingers for a moment and sent rivulets of energy up her arm.

He looked closer at the ring. "This was why you wound up at that Pawn Shop wasn't it?"

She nodded "I think Tasha might have thought I pawned it. She turned cold and silent toward the end of last week."

"So, whatever happened on Saturday changed her mind. She sent you the ring because someone frightened her."

Dani choked back a tear. She understood the terror that must have filled Tasha's chest, tightening around her heart and lungs until they felt ready to burst. "She called someone at your department and made an appointment."

"And she thought it was me she was talking to." He pulled back into the street and crawled toward a halted intersection. "Did she keep the appointment?"

"She'd know it wasn't you, but if she met with another policeman, she might not have been concerned." Her voice broke slightly.

Jay locked eyes with her. "Can I keep this?"

"Why?" She studied him. She wanted to trust him. Wanted to have someone with skin on that she could believe in.

He held up a finger and, with his other hand, punched in a code on a panel next to his radio. A mechanism clicked and a small section of the dash swung open exposing a hidden opening with his weapon inside. "This is locked unless I unlock it. No one has the combination except me."

She bit her lip. The place certainly seemed more secure than her satchel. She glanced from the opening to Jay's dark gaze.

"I promise, I won't let anyone else in on this, and I'll keep the ring safe."

She dropped her head in a nod. He tugged out

his gun and laid the tiny ring in its place before closing the panel. He climbed from the car. Immediately, his dark hair shuddered from the wind. The gale blasted through his open door and wrapped around her in a frigid grip. The temperature must have dropped twenty degrees since she'd traveled with Tyrone and Carla to dinner.

Jay rounded the back of the car and opened the trunk again. Surely not to retrieve his dirty clothes, though she couldn't fathom what might be back there. She unlatched her belt about the time he opened her door. "I'll walk you up."

"That isn't necessary."

"I know." He held out his hand.

Not to be rude, Dani laid hers in his palm. But the tingles of electricity along her arm and down her back confessed her growing attraction to this man. An instantaneous pang when he dropped her hand confirmed the matter.

Jay unfolded a rough wool blanket and wrapped it around her shoulders. "Not cuddly, but decidedly warm, huh?" He kept his hand at her back.

"Thanks. I feel guilty, though. You must be freezing."

"I like the cold."

They walked in silence up the open stairs. Jay paused at the top. He put his hands on her shoulders, his dark eyes piercing hers. "I'm glad you trusted me tonight, Dani. I'll do everything I can to find your friend."

"I believe you." Did she truly? With every fiber of her being she wanted to. Yet her dad's voice about her trusting nature echoed through her mind. Add to that, her history of putting her faith in different men.

Lord, you know the truth about Jay's heart. Don't let me place my trust unwisely.

"You have to know this means someone, likely one of my co-workers, might have had a hand in this."

"It happens." She broke her gaze and looked down. She'd seen it before. One of Dad's best friends. "People are people, whether cops, clergy, or businessmen. They don't become all-perfect superheroes just because they take on a job."

"You sound a little cynical." He rubbed her shoulders.

"I don't put people on pedestals. Everyone blows it from time to time." Especially her.

He nodded. "Don't speak to anyone else at the

department about this. I'm not sure who you can trust."

She lifted her gaze and caught his. "I trust you."

He gave a half smile. "Thanks for that." He stroked her cheek with his thumb.

An electrical volt trickled at his touch. She leaned into it.

Something like shock crossed over his eyes. He backed away, giving a path to her door. "I'll say goodnight, then."

Dani sighed. Way too close for comfort there. She took a few steps toward her apartment and halted. The door. Someone had…. "Um, Jay?"

He came closer, his eyes fixed on the gap of darkness separating her door from the frame. With one hand he reached for his weapon while nudging her to the side of her entrance. With the toe of his shoe, he pushed the door wider.

Grime Beat

Chapter Nine

Jay hugged the wall next to the open door.

Dani stood beside him. "The light switch." Her warm whisper tickled his neck. "It's on the opposite door facing."

Lights, good thinking. He counted to an internal three and took a deep breath. In one fluid motion, he flicked on the light with one hand and crouched, aiming his weapon toward the center of the room.

Devastation. Every item broken, torn. Shattered glass from a bookcase mingled with shards from an empty wrought iron mirror. Stuffing from throw pillows and a wingback chair mingled with a broken flat-screen TV. Books, lamps, and DVDs added to the litter on the floor.

But no movement. He motioned for Dani to remain where she was and kept his back to the wall as he made his way to the bedroom. Again, the door stood open. He peeked across the doorway for an instant. More destruction. He found no sign of the person who had made the mess.

He flicked on the light and examined the room, checking the closet and under the bed. A breeze billowed the heavy drapes over her patio door. He eyed the empty porch. Glass littered the inside of the door. A likely entry point. He'd need to get his kit and check the remaining glass for traces of skin or blood.

Circling the room, he exited and opened the tiny bathroom wide before he made his way into the mess in the small kitchen. Same scene there, the floor filled with the contents of the cabinets, freezer, and fridge. "Clear."

Dani gasped as she stepped into the mess. "Agh." She let the blanket drop at her ankles.

"Don't touch anything." He picked his way across the wide area that served as the living and dining rooms.

Dani started to retrieve a broken trinket and clasped her hands at her chest. "I can't do this again."

Again? She probably referred to Tasha's apartment. "Dani, I'm sorry."

She pushed past him into her bedroom, what was left of it, with Jay at her heels. The mattress, ripped open, leaned against one wall. The contents of her drawers and closet lay in the center of the box spring along with destroyed pictures from the wall, an emptied jewelry box, torn books, and a ripped-up teddy bear.

"No." She sank to her knees next to a shattered frame and the remains of a shredded photograph. She reached for the pieces and drew her hand back as a tiny sob escaped.

He pulled her to her feet and wrapped his arms around her slender shoulders. As she gulped in broken breaths, he absorbed her pain.

"It's all I have left."

He rubbed her back and tucked her head under his chin.

She gripped the front of his tee shirt. "Why is this happening to me, again?"

What was she talking about? "Again?"

Stiffening in his arms, she released her hold. "No." She stepped back and rubbed her sleeve across her eyes leaving a dark streak on the fabric of her dress.

"Wait." Jay lifted a cup-towel from the box spring and handed it to her. "No need to ruin your dress. It's made it this far." He mustered a smile, but she didn't respond.

She drew the fabric under her eyelids. "I'm sorry. I don't usually lose it like this."

"No need to apologize." Untangling a pile of clothes and hangers, he separated a jacket from the group. He held it for her, and she slipped her arms through the sleeves.

"Thank you, but I'll be fine."

"Ha. You're funny in the head if you think I'm going to let you stay in this wreck."

"I...." She did a slow rotation and put her hands to her head. "I have nowhere else to go. I need to make a phone call."

"Stop, Dani." He encircled her waist and halted her turn. "I'll take care of you. Just trust me."

"I don't know who to trust."

"Yes, you do." He drew her closer and aimed for the front door. "You've already decided to trust me. That's why you gave me the ring. And I've given you my promise." He pushed her out the entrance, followed a half step behind, and used the edge of his tee shirt to pull the door firmly shut. "I'll come back tomorrow and scan the scene."

"What about the police?"

He let the question hang until they'd gotten back into his car. The thought made him sick, but he couldn't fathom another option. "Someone at the department has to be involved. I'd rather do some investigating on my own until I can figure out who's legit."

Dani pulled her legs under her in the seat, staring out the passenger window.

"Don't worry." He paused at the turn-off to look at her. "You aren't going to disappear."

Disappear? Déjà vu again. Dani shoved the image of her dad's ruined picture into the back of her mind. She needed to speak to Matthew. Maybe he'd believe her now.

But truth be told, she had more faith in Jay than she did in Matt. And Jay knew nothing of her life before Dallas, or what brought her here. "Where are you taking me?"

She glanced at his strong profile, his hair still

mussed from the wind and a tiny wrinkle across his forehead, as he stared through the windshield. His blanket had been left behind in her apartment. She'd have to make that up to him. Though she couldn't repay him for the comfort of not having to arrive at that scene alone.

"There's a hotel not far from my house. I don't expect you to have any more trouble, but I want to be close if there is."

"You're not responsible for me."

He looked at her then. "True. But you don't seem to have anyone else at this point, and I'm willing."

Her mind screamed at her not to reply. She needed to embrace the kindness and be grateful without insisting on her independence. Because he was right. She didn't have anyone else. Not anyone who knew where she was anyway.

"I need you to think back to the crime scene where you found this ring."

"It was under the bottom veneer of the dresser. We wouldn't have found it at all if we didn't move the furniture to clean the carpet." His scowl clearly revealed how missing that evidence bugged him still.

"But who turned it over? Which one of you?"

"Frank always turns in collected evidence." She ran her hand along the smooth tan leather that made the ridge under the window.

Jay heaved a sigh. "Then he's probably the one who pawned the ring."

"Wait, he didn't turn it in that day. He had another appointment. He gave the package to me." That sure explained things. "That's probably why Tasha was so cold around me last Friday. She found the ring and remembered that I got the satchel from Frank."

"She thought you must have been the one to pawn the ring. But if you didn't, then who did?"

Dani stared out the window as they drove through a mix-master at I-35. Jay wouldn't like her answer. "I gave it to Tyrone. He's team lead, so he should have been the one to get it. But Frank wouldn't have given it to him. He won't even speak to him. I think the man is scared of Tyrone."

Jay growled. Obviously, he didn't like the conclusion any more than she did.

"You can't think he had anything to do with this."

"I have to, Dani. My own partner is in the suspect pool." He wiped his hand over his face. "Anyone who touched that evidence before it reached lock-up might have taken the ring. I'll know more when I get to the department." He cut his eyes toward her for a second. "Was there anything else of value in the things I missed?"

She hated that he felt guilty over the issue. What had been in that package besides the ring? Just discarded tissues as far as she knew. "Not that I can remember."

"I'll be able to learn more when I look at the evidence log tomorrow." He took the Belt Line exit and drove through the spine of one of the suburbs several miles north of her home.

"What about my apartment?"

"I'll go over there after I take you in to work. I'll see if Carla can bring you back from your job site." He rubbed a finger across his chin. "I can't believe that Tyrone has anything to do with this, but I know he won't act with his wife around. I'll have her stay with you until I can return."

Babysitter. She shut her eyes for a moment but didn't turn away from him. He'd done so much for her. But without a car, she had no escape. The straitjacket began to tighten.

"Can't I get my car in the morning?"

He stopped at a well-lit intersection and turned toward her while the traffic signal held them up. "Tasha is gone. I don't know why or by whose hand, but I don't want the same thing to happen to you. And your home looks way too much like Tasha's did."

He was right. Exactly. Down to the open carton of milk spilling its contents on her kitchen floor.

"I know." She focused on her lap and willed her tears to stay back. "Part of me just wants to get on I-30 and go west until I drop into the ocean."

"Running doesn't usually solve anything." He rubbed her shoulder. "I'm not one for taking that route. I'd rather face the trouble than have it always haunting me."

He had no idea how that felt.

Jay parked in front of a Garden Inn. He accompanied her to the desk and insisted on paying for the room before he left with barely a goodbye. She waved at his back then meandered through the hallways to find her new little corner of the world.

Number 116. Where was it? Images of her living room, her bedroom, flashed through her mind. She took a right down the corridor and tried to sweep away the emotions, but there were too many. Too much pain. Her mom's ballerina dancer. Her dad's picture.

Where was her stupid room? She spotted the number and shoved the keycard into the slot. Once again, everything that was her life had been ruined. Not left bleeding on the carpet but just as destroyed. Now where would she run?

Yes, run. She sure couldn't stand and face an invisible enemy who sneaks into homes and shoots from abandoned buildings.

She sniffed and glanced at the clock. The wee hours of the morning kept her from calling Matthew. He deserved to lose a little sleep, but for now she was safe enough. Better to not waste her last, best defense when she didn't really need it.

And then again, if she caught him during business hours and in a good mood, if she held her mouth just right, he'd lift a finger to help her. But she wouldn't wager much on that prospect.

Why is this happening to me, God? Again? He could handle her questions, but as much as she wished for one, He didn't owe her an answer.

After washing her face, she pulled the sheets of the bed back. Should she sleep in her dress or shed it? What she wouldn't give for a pair of socks.

A knock sounded, making her jump. Who?

She peered through the eye-level hole and saw Jay's face on the other side. She opened the door. "What are you doing back here?"

"Necessities. I'm not so hot on sizes, but I think you can get along with these." He hoisted Wal-Mart bags onto the dresser then turned his back on her.

"Wait." She caught him by the arm as he pulled the door open. Without thinking, she threw her arms around his neck in a bear hug. "I can't thank you enough for all of this. I don't know what I would've done…."

He returned her embrace for a moment, then released her and stepped into the hallway. "I'm just glad you weren't alone. I'll come get you in the morning."

She let the door close behind him. What was she thinking, embracing him like that? Emotional. Irrational. Thankfully, he hadn't seemed to respond.

And that was a good thing, right?

Grime Beat

Chapter Ten

Jay cranked up the heat when he entered his house. His yellow lab padded in from the small, brown-grass lot beyond the dog door, and his beagle looked up from where she lay on the couch. "Hey, guys." He patted each head and made for the shower. Shivering, he let the warm water wash over him and get his blood flowing again into his fingers and toes.

Dani filled his mind. The way she took care of Marv's wife. How she wrapped her coat around that teenager. Her ability to laugh at herself during dinner. Then there was the embrace she gave him.

That alone erased his embarrassment at his eager acceptance of Carla's invitation for them to come to dinner on Friday. As to that, he didn't remember Dani actually accepting it.

Instead of letting his stupidity distract him, he should be thinking about ways to track Tasha.

Sadie whined at the bathroom door. "In a second, girl." His beagle was always hungry. Would literally march him out to the food bin at mealtimes.

"Wish I could be so focused." His job, whatever the chances were of his promotion, relied on his ability to have singularity of thought. A narrowed scope. But with Tasha's situation, he'd actually be investigating his own team members. Even Cal.

If he took this step, he might as well wave goodbye to the supervisor's position. Might even have to give up the force altogether and get his P.I. license. The hideous thought hit him like a wave of cold water.

An hour later, he lay in bed staring at the ceiling. His thoughts still spun. Someone… someone on his team had stolen a piece of evidence—valuable if not truly important—and that same person might very well be involved in the disappearance of a young woman, the trashing of her apartment. And Dani's.

He couldn't let Dani get hurt. Or disappear.

Giving up, he dressed and drove to his station, not far from Dani's hotel. At least she could sleep in security.

"What are you doing here so late?" Kirkland spotted him almost as soon as he entered. "Or should I say early?"

"Bothered about something. Might as well try to work through it since it's stealing my sleep." Jay flicked on his computer and waited for it to boot.

"I know what you mean. Doing the night shift can get burdensome, but at least most of the problems are solved during the day so I don't have to worry about them." The seasoned cop moved closer. "So what's eating you?"

Jay shook his head. "Details that should fit but don't."

He wouldn't mention Dani's name. Not even to Kirkland, though the man had been at the department longer than almost anyone else. Nearing retirement age, his dream was to move out to the piece of land he used as a hunting lease in East Texas near Lake Fork.

"Y'all have fun this weekend?"

"Great time. Just me and Hall, though. Cal didn't end up coming. Said something about a previous commitment." The cop wiped his graying eyebrows.

Really? Sunday, Cal had met him and a few others to watch the NFL playoffs, Denver against Green Bay. Jay had the distinct impression that he'd come directly from the lake. Another troubling issue. "Glad you two had fun."

He turned to his desk and waited for Kirkland to move away.

With the solitude, Jay opened a file from the call he and Cal had worked. The one where Dani claimed the ring originated. Of course, he hadn't seen it, so it wasn't in the record, but he looked through the report for any other valuable items. Several. Pearl pieces, some pin with a large ruby. At least it had looked like a ruby, though he was no expert. He scanned the list of names on the trail of evidence. Not too many had touched this case, especially after the medical examiner's ruling. Jay and his partner, Cal, of course. He figured he'd have to include his supervisor, Lieutenant Gates among his suspects. Then Tyrone's name was on the sheet, though he still had trouble accepting that prospect.

And there wasn't a record of who had received Tyrone's evidence. Go figure.

He pushed away from his desk and carried the slim file downstairs. After scratching his signature in the book outside of the evidence lock-up, he waved to the guard on duty. "Hey, Todd. Can you tell me who was on duty down here when addendum #88825 came in this month?"

Officer Todd pushed a button that allowed his entrance. "Hang on." The young man's hands skimmed the keyboard. By the looks of his speed on the computer, he'd probably done more typing than writing with a pen. "January fourth, 17:51. Looks like Hall had the desk."

"Does your record say who brought the evidence to him?"

"Hmm. That should be here." He frowned. "Huge breach in protocol. But I sure don't see any name."

No surprise there. He'd have to talk to Hall when he got the chance. He thanked the man and strolled to the shelves. The box he sought topped one of the stacks. A contents list lay on the top of the various packages. Odd that none of the items were marked for return. Usually, for a suicide, they would go to the next of kin with the coroner's report.

Kellerman's container was under the initial

sheet. He opened the satchel and tugged out the inventory list. Had this even been examined? He saw no signs that it had, but why would it, since the victim killed herself?

The items were written in a female's manuscript. Dani's? Whether her or Tasha, she should have known better than to use pencil, but then according to Dani, Frank was the one who normally filled all of this out.

The ring wasn't listed. He grimaced. She'd seemed so sure.

What was listed seemed like random items: a used tissue, a single driving glove, an earring with a missing back, a pepper shaker. Strange there wasn't a saltshaker to go with it. And why had Dani skipped every other numbered line?

He checked out the box and returned to his desk.

Using a magnifying glass, he examined the paper. Residue from erased lines appeared in the gaps. Hard to see, but the glass picked it up. A scope would pick up even more, but that would take submitting it to one of the data analysts. Better to glean as much as he could before talking to anyone else.

The nearly erased lines revealed that there had

been a second earring and a saltshaker. At least two other entries had been too thoroughly deleted to leave a hint of what they had said.

He dug through the container. Of course, no ring came to light, but he only had Dani's word that she'd found it. That she'd seen it be submitted with the rest of the possible evidence. She could have made a mistake.

Though that would mean Tasha was wrong as well. If that were true, why had she disappeared? Who trashed the apartments and why?

Tyrone was already on his list of suspects. Jay shook his head. Tyrone was the most honest, sincere man he knew. Surely, he had no part in the ring's sale or in Tasha's disappearance.

But if both women were right about the ring, it cemented Tyrone's place on the list. And if they found something to further prove foul play in Tasha's disappearance, the detectives would take a hard look at his friend. No one would need to work too hard to build a case against him with a possible motive, his unique position of gleaning information, and the likely opportunity he had.

That possibility still didn't answer who had turned the box in at the evidence lock up.

Just after dawn, Cal arrived.

Jay cut his eyes toward him. "Early for you, isn't it?"

Cal grimaced. "I… that is…." He took a bite of a bagel. "Want one?"

"Nah. Thanks." Jay's stomach rumbled. Good excuse to dash out and avoid any potential questions. Besides, he wanted to meet Dani at her hotel for breakfast. Maybe chat for a while before he took her to Kellerman's.

He slipped into his leather jacket on his way to the door and turned back to wave at Cal. The man's face looked several shades paler than normal. Shoulders up, he glanced around him as he reached for his office phone.

What was he up to?

Sleep had been a joke. If her dreams weren't filled with shadows chasing her or glimpses of Tasha's panicked face, her long periods of wakefulness and drowsiness were plagued with conflicting feelings about Jay. He was still the most logical suspect in Tasha's disappearance, but Dani was sure he had nothing to do with it. Or with the ring.

If only she had some reason for that confidence besides her attraction to him.

But that's all it was. Attraction. Infatuation at best. Stirred up due to his physique in that tight tee shirt, his rush to assist Marv at the accident, and his gentle protection of her last night. So attentive. So compassionate.

Agh. If she didn't clear her thoughts of him, she'd be completely worthless today. Especially on top of having no sleep. Besides, her record with men, especially good guys who could never do wrong, was ridiculous.

She had to maintain distance with him. Nice. Polite. Detached. Not interested.

When dawn finally lit the bottom of the heavy curtains, she rose and gazed in the mirror. Dark circles under her eyes gave her a zombie appearance. Great. Jay would be picking her up in the next hour or so, and she looked like an extra on The Walking Dead.

After gripping her hair into her normal bun, she gave up on the rest of her appearance and let the amazing smells of the dining room draw her. Looks aside, she'd feel better after she ate.

She followed her nose down the main corridor and out into the large foyer. The far third of it was separated by a wide cabinet and randomly spaced lattices holding lamps and well-dusted fake plants. Aromas of bacon and waffles enticed her forward. She slipped between two cream colored sections of modified wall.

"Good morning to you, miss." An elderly man, Creole if she attributed the accent correctly, greeted her. His starched shirt had a tag identifying him as Max. He squinted and adjusted the white chef's cap on his head. "I'll be thinking you're a fan of omelets, nez-pah?"

"Mmm. What do you suggest?"

"Hm." He hooked a finger at the corner of his mouth. "Bacon." His finger pointed as punctuation and rehooked.

Yum, but how had he gotten that from staring at her?

"Colby Jack cheese." Again, the finger straightened before returning to its place between his lips.

"My favorite. How did you know?"

"Ah, yes, tiny shallots with chunks of ham and diced tomatoes with a little green pepper." This time both hands came to the sides of his face, his pointers and thumbs in matching *Okay* symbols. "Very mild. Maybe a splash of sour cream on the side, no?"

Heaven. "That sounds amazing."

He winked and snapped his finger then marched toward what must have been the kitchen entrance.

While he created his masterpiece, she wandered toward the tall dividers. On the back side, they just looked like cabinets, but on this side, they held all sorts of breads and beverages. She spotted a waffle iron next to a basket of Danishes. She helped herself to a cup of batter, poured it onto the heated press, and turned the timer on. The enticing smell, at least one of them, originated from this press.

She turned. About a dozen or so quad tables filled the section, all in the same style as the lattice. The wicker chairs gave a feeling of a southern veranda, and fresh flowers in the center of starched tablecloths offered formal comfort.

A thirty-something guy had his laptop and several files spread across one table. He let his full plate chill while he pounded the keypad and spoke curses under his breath.

Another man, roughly forty, dallied over the newspaper. A bowl and two plates surrounded him with one holding a remaining crust from a piece of toast. He glanced up and smiled when he caught her gaze.

She looked away, and the timer beeped on her waffle. She buttered and dressed it with cinnamon, blueberries, and a smattering of syrup before she sat at a table in the corner.

Max brought her omelet. "You will like." He tipped his hat before greeting a trio of new arrivals.

She hadn't felt this at ease since Tasha had gone missing. She bowed her head and thanked the Lord for her current safety, for Jay's continued help, and for the delicious food. Hopefully, it tasted as good as it smelled.

The meal was even better than expected. Cheese and bacon mingled with spices he hadn't mentioned. She ate about half of her dish and several bites of the waffle before giving up. What a shame she couldn't bag it for lunch.

She pulled out her phone and stroked through her messages. Still nothing from Tasha. What did she expect? But she didn't want to encourage the fear to return. Without her Bible or her study book, she opened her reading app and flipped to 2 Timothy where her new study was about to start. If she couldn't do the lesson, at least she could read through the chapter.

The seventh verse captured her. "For God hath not given us the spirit of fear; but of power, and of love, and of a sound mind."

A mallet wouldn't have made a bigger impact.

The spirit of fear had been with her since she'd arrived in Dallas. Most of the last four months at least. And with Tasha's disappearance, it had been more like a spirit of terror than everyday fear.

And she sure hadn't used sound judgment when she went scaling walls and rooftops. Hadn't spent a second even thinking through possible outcomes. Of course, ending up at the police station would not likely have been on her list.

She glanced up as the main doors opened. Had she sensed Jay's presence? She'd paid no attention to other arrivals, yet she saw his swagger immediately. She must have subconsciously noticed him outside the windows. That didn't explain why her chest convulsed when he caught her eye and smiled. All her intentions to maintain a polite but distant relationship fled as he joined her at the table.

"Sleep well?"

She nodded. Did lies count when they weren't exactly spoken?

"Well, I didn't. Finding out who might have had access to the ring Tasha sent you stayed at the forefront of my mind."

"Oh. I'm so sorry."

He sat across from her and waved his hand. "Don't be. Bothered me 'til I did something about it. Found out that there's a gap in the logbook. I don't have a record of who Tyrone gave the evidence to."

"Have you asked him?"

He glanced at his watch. "Still too early. Thought I'd talk to him when I drop you off."

Max approached. "Can I build a Max-special platter for you, sir?"

"Thanks, but no." He held out an empty cup. "But I'd love some coffee."

"Coming right up." Max filled it from a carafe and gave Dani a thumbs up. "You like?"

She smiled and her cheeks warmed. Yes, but she wouldn't give Jay any hint that she felt that way. Oh wait, he was talking about the omelet.

Pull it together, Dani. She put her eyes on her plate and toyed with a final bite she couldn't conceive of stuffing into her belly. Focus—Tasha, the ring, evidence bag. "I don't remember having evidence from any other crime scene recently. Surely Tyrone will remember."

"I hope he can do better than Ethan Hall." Jay sipped his coffee. "He's the day clerk at the evidence lock-up. You'd think he'd notice a missing entry, might remember something about getting the satchel. But no. He couldn't tell me a thing about it."

"Yet he's in such a responsible position? I'd think a good memory and observation skills, especially for the details of the normal paperwork, would be crucial for someone in his position."

"And he's usually got all of that, but the stuff y'all turn in isn't quite as secured. The various cleaning companies do reports their own ways, even though they have formal instructions from us. Things aren't secure until they get into the lock up."

"Then get the feed from the cameras. You'll see whoever it was turning in the satchel."

He sipped again. "Yeah, a possibility. But I'd have to make a report to the Internal Assistant Director to do that."

"Okay…." So? She didn't want to be rude, but what was the big deal with writing up a simple report?

"It's not that easy, Dani." He set his mug down and pushed it away. "I'm a cop. If I'm going to make the slightest hint that another officer made a mistake or is dirty, I better have some pretty strong evidence to back it up. At this point, there are too many suspects, and none of them have motives. In fact, the only reason they are under suspicion is because of proximity to the evidence."

"Well, who wasn't on duty between last Saturday night and Monday morning?"

"Where did you come up with the time period?"

Dani shifted. At this moment, she couldn't be the detective's daughter that she was. "Assumptions. Whoever pawned the ring either grabbed Tasha or chased her off, right?"

"Safe enough. Wait, I get it. You got the package when? Tuesday? It had to be mailed by Monday's first collection."

"Eleven in the morning, but probably before then or she would have come into work."

"Duly noted. But why is Saturday night the earliest time?"

"Last pickup on Saturday is five in the afternoon. Had she mailed it earlier, I would have received it on Monday."

He blinked. "Brilliant deduction, Watson."

She grinned. "I guess that makes you Sherlock?"

He stuck his thumb under his jacket collar. "Of course. But that still leaves a number of suspects. With me still at the top of the list, I bet."

Not on hers. She didn't meet his eyes. "Were you off on Sunday?"

"All day. And I had access to the lock-up."

"If you're the guy…." She made eye contact. "Tyrone will certainly remember."

"I'll let you talk to him, then. Put your mind at ease." He threw a five-dollar bill on the table and stood.

She followed him to the lot and climbed into his Charger. "If you are the guy, Sherlock, you've got lousy aim." Oh wait, she hadn't mentioned that detail.

He paused, his hand on the ignition key. His head whipped around. "Excuse me?"

She'd meant to lighten the mood with a joking jab. Total failure. "I… uh…."

"What are you not telling me?" He draped his arm over the back of her seat.

The action wasn't affectionate. His stormy

attitude verified that much. Along with the wrinkle in between his furrowed brows.

She hesitated for a long moment. He'd be angry that she hadn't confessed before. Angry that she'd even gone to the pawn shop in the first place.

"Well, when I got Tasha's note, I thought I'd visit the place she mentioned."

"I know all about that. And I heard about the call, but the cops found no one to verify any shooting."

"I wasn't going to stick around." Not near some crazy man with a gun and fairly good aim.

"Fine, but you didn't tell me someone shot at you."

"It didn't seem important."

"Are you kidding? You could have been… hurt. Badly hurt." His eyes softened for a moment before he turned the key and scanned the area with his mirrors. Silence settled for several minutes until the trip brought them to normal, Dallas morning traffic on busy Belt Line Road.

"Did you see the shooter?"

"Only a glimpse. Man, I think, but in bulky clothes. Hard to know for sure." They passed restaurants blurred into the gray background of yet

Marji Laine

another cloudy sky.

A muscle on the side of his jaw pumped. "How many shots?"

She focused on the tan dashboard in front of her and tried to concentrate. "Three at least. I'm not sure beyond that. I couldn't hear them."

"Then why do you think the guy was shooting? Did you see a gun?"

He sounded like Matthew. Why did men always assume that she didn't have a half-brain in her head? "Didn't have to. The window of the car next to me shattered. The glass behind me got a new hole."

The muscle tensed again. "Anyone else hear it or see the guy?"

Was her word not good enough? She brushed the thought aside and stared out her window. The restaurants had given way to cheap apartments bordered by a commuter train station. "The man in Pete's was ducking for cover in his back room. And he'd taken a long time supposedly finding information about the ring. Well, finding out that he had no information about it."

A red light at the freeway intersection halted their progress. "He made a call." Jay's eyes narrowed.

Her thoughts exactly. Her annoyance subsided. He wasn't questioning her observations and conclusions. He was just thinking like a cop. A second witness would support her statements.

He grimaced. "You should have told me."

"I…." She sighed. He was right. "I'm sorry. Things have been happening so fast."

He turned, catching her with his penetrating, dark eyes. They should have pierced her through, yet a line of worry between his brows softened them. "And someone tried to kill you."

Did he have to put it quite that way? "He didn't, though."

Jay took I-35 south, and quiet surrounded them for a while. Well, the relative quiet of a stop and go freeway, disregarding the squeaking brakes of a cargo truck beside them and the occasional heavy base pounding from passing cars.

Before too long, Jay parked in front of Kellerman's and turned his full attention to her, his gaze soft with kindness and concern.

A ripple of nervous anticipation scuttled up her spine. What was happening to her? She'd set aside men for good after her last catastrophe. Yet this… oh. He was… so perfect.

He licked his lips. "That shooter better not

have another chance, Dani. Or he might succeed."

She flinched. Way to turn her warm, mellow thoughts into popsicles. "I understand." Did she? Hadn't she had a discussion exactly like this several months ago?

Touching the release of his safety belt, he shifted in his seat. "I hope so. Now what else have you neglected to tell me?"

Chapter Eleven

Dani's information confirmed Jay's suspicions. He had some digging to do.

Tyrone arrived, ending their discussion. The knowing look in his eye raised Jay's defenses. He and Dani had been leaning against the passenger side of his car, but he stepped away and crossed his arms.

"Morning, you two." The man's natural smile held a hint of victory.

Hate to squash your pride, there, sport. "I've got a police question for you, Tyrone."

The smile ebbed.

That's right. Nothing but official duty here.

Jay explained about the satchel that Tyrone had turned in. He remembered the situation but gave no help as to the identity of the man who took possession of it. "Just some beat cop, as far as I could tell."

"Beat cop?"

"Yeah, uniform. I'd never seen him before. And I couldn't remember his name to save my life."

If he'd known it might save Dani's or Tasha's, would he have worked harder to remember? Better to not to go there. The last thing Jay needed was some well-meaning friend to try investigating. He had his hands full with Dani already.

He said goodbye and headed toward his office, mulling over possibilities. One thing was certain from her revelations—subtlety was no longer an option. If he had to go through official channels, talk to his superiors or Internal Affairs, he would.

And kiss his possible promotion goodbye.

Reaching the station, he cornered Cal in the break room. The man chomped on a chocolate chip cookie. He always had some snack hanging from his mouth. How he stayed in shape, Jay couldn't figure.

"Want some?" Crumbs fell from his bottom

lip.

He still hadn't eaten. And maybe if he joined his partner, the mood could stay light enough to get the information he needed without ticking Cal off.

He took a few. Leaning against the counter between the sink and the fridge, he ate through one in silence.

Cal spoke through the cookie morsels. "What's on your mind, kid?"

The slight didn't bother him nearly as much now as it did when he first joined the force. Maybe because only his partner would call a man Jay's age kid. "We go back a long way, Cal." Jay's entire career.

"Yep. Since you were a twig, fresh outta the academy." A tiny tremor shook his hand and the faintest fever tinged his cheeks.

"Something you need to tell me?" Jay consumed another cookie. Two female officers came in chatting about some new movie slated to open this weekend. He kept his eyes on Cal until the women exited.

His partner returned the stare, continuing to chew slowly through one sweet at a time. Probably inhaled six by the time they had the break room to themselves again.

"Well?" Jay crossed his arms.

The older man halted, a final bite halfway to his mouth. He lowered his hand. "What are you getting at?"

"Where were you this Sunday? You told me you were going to the lake with Kirkland, but he said you never showed."

A vein in Cal's neck bulged. "Plans change."

Not good enough. "So where were you?"

"I suppose Kirkland and Hall are ganging up on me, huh?" He tossed the last chunk into the sink. "I knew this couldn't last."

"What's that?"

He pointed a bony finger at Jay's face. "Look, kid. This doesn't have anything to do with you. Stay out of it. You hear me?"

"Cal...."

He stomped from the room muttering expletives. "Leave me alone."

Jay wandered to the food Cal left. He picked up the package of cookies and uncovered Cal's cell phone. He thought he had heard the man speaking to someone when he first came in but decided he'd been mistaken. He stared at the line. Still open. Still on speaker. He pushed a button to retrieve the call information.

Miranda Hall?

Jay recoiled at the porch of the Hall home. What was he doing? Cal wasn't the brightest to be calling a co-worker's wife, but the act certainly wasn't criminal.

Follow the leads. Drilled in advice. Even if Hall's wife turned out to be inconsequential, he needed to know where Cal had been this weekend. If for no other reason than to remove his partner from the suspect list. He stared at the mat in front of the door. *Happily Ever After* splayed across an imprint of Sleeping Beauty's castle. His questions might destroy that dream for the Halls.

He pushed the door button. Chimes like his mom's grandfather clock echoed through the house. *Guide my questions, Lord.* He had to stay on-track or risk messing up this investigation. Not to mention the chance of losing a friend and undoing the positive spiritual strides he'd made. Cal hadn't fully grasped the concepts of faith, but at least he'd been thinking about God lately.

A woman opened the door and greeted him

with a quizzical look and a half-smile. Her dark hair bobbed with the vitality of youth. "I know you. You're one of the cops at the station. What are you doing here?"

"Can I speak to you for a second?"

"Sure. Come on in." She smoothed her hands over her trim, cream-colored slacks.

Though way too young for Cal, Jay could understand why his partner might have been enticed. He eyed her low-cut pink sweater for a nanosecond. "It won't take long. Can we sit out here?"

She glanced at the sky and grimaced. Jay wasn't about to go inside. He silently stood with his arms crossed, leaning against the white rail of her porch.

After a hesitation, she huffed and disappeared into the house, leaving the front door ajar.

He smiled inwardly and examined the two-story ranch. Red brick with white accents. Nice place. Wide lawn, new area. Mrs. Hall must have a good-paying job because Ethan's salary sure didn't finance this place.

Carrying an over-sized hoodie, she returned to the porch. "What is it you want?" She slipped the thick material over her head and settled in the white-washed rocker opposite him. She tilted her chin, glancing at him through the corners of her eyes. Almost a seductive model pose. Her act was obvious.

He held out his hand. "Jay. Jay Hunter."

"All right." She shook and waved a hand to the wicker chair beside her. "Sit."

He thanked her and claimed the seat. "I'm trying to figure out some things. Details of a case I'm working on."

"And you suspect I have something to do with it? That's rather ridiculous, don't you think?" She adjusted in her chair and smiled.

"Actually, it's not you I'm asking about."

Her smile vanished. She crossed her legs and pulled the hoodie around her. "Well, if you want to know what Ethan's got himself into, you'll have to talk to him. I rarely see the man. He never comes home anymore." She leaned against the chair back.

From the sound of things, trouble with happily-ever-after came long before Jay arrived. "He's not the one I need to ask about either."

Her head straightened, and her features hardened. "Who else could I possibly report on? If you want gossip, I suggest a visit to the hair salon down the street, or maybe a copy of one of the magazines at the grocery checkout lane." Her volume grew.

"I was thinking about my partner, Calvin Cutter. I think you know him?"

"I know a lot of people." She lowered her voice and kept her eyes level.

"You know him better than some. Better than most, probably."

"And what's that supposed to mean?"

He put up his hands. "I'm not looking for trouble, Mrs. Hall. Not for you and not for Cal. I just want to know if he happened to spend time with you last Sunday. He wasn't at the fishing trip with your husband and Kirkland."

"And with nothing more than that...." She abruptly crossed her arms. "You come here and start making insinuations. How dare...."

With a roar of an engine and a squeal of tires, Cal pulled his brown Chevy into the drive. He bolted from the car. "What are you doing here, Hunter?"

Lousy timing. "I could ask you the same. But I think I already know the answer."

"This is none of your business." He leapt onto the porch, skipping the two steps altogether, and slammed his palm against one of the wooden pillars.

"I said the same thing." Miranda Hall wiggled her hanging foot.

Jay stood. "You're right. I only want to know if you were here while Kirkland and Hall were fishing Lake Fork this weekend. You told me you'd been with them, but I know you were lying."

His partner worked his jaw. "I knew this couldn't last."

"So you were here this weekend." He glanced from his partner's contrite face to the lifted chin of the woman seated.

"You don't have to tell him anything." Miranda Hall glared up at him

"I came here to break things off. I can't do this." The man had aged ten years in the time since he and Jay had spoken in the break room. "This isn't right. I told you that from the beginning."

Her face turned scarlet.

He stared at the ground. "As for Jay, he must have a good reason for asking. I trust him."

She jumped up. "Yeah? Well, I don't. So help me, Jay Hunter, if I hear anything disagreeable from that cheating husband of mine, I'll be after you with the business end of my lawn trimmer." She stomped her foot.

"Cheating?" Jay should have stopped while he had the chance.

"Yes, cheating." Her eyes sparked with hate. "Probably has some strumpet at that apartment of his."

"He has an apartment?"

Cal nodded. "Across from City Place down on Haskell."

Jay didn't ask why Cal would know that. How did a cop Ethan's age afford a suburban home like this and a downtown apartment?

Miranda scowled. "And as for his stupid fishing trip, I don't know how he got Kirkland to lie for him, but every stinking one of his fish was still frozen inside. He didn't even try to make them seem fresh caught. Like I'm so stupid I wouldn't notice."

She pushed through her door and slammed it in Cal's face as he tried to follow her.

"I'm sorry." Jay's apology only got a partial glance from his partner.

"I hope you had a good reason for this." Cal stepped off the porch.

Jay tracked him across the yard. "I do. But let me be clear, you were with Miranda Hall on Sunday?"

Cal stopped and faced him. "From noon on Saturday until almost five Sunday afternoon. Then I met you and the others at Griff's for the football game."

Jay nodded.

Cal planted his finger against Jay's chest. "See to it that no one else hears about this. Got it?"

He didn't respond. Couldn't make that promise, though he would do his best to keep the information under wraps. Still, his and Cal's friendship would never be the same. And it would be non-existent if he had to mention anything about the relationship the man had just ended with Miranda Hall. Hopefully, the investigation would avoid that area completely.

Dani pulled the edges of heavy fabric across the exposed cushion of her cheap couch and attempted to stitch the gaping pieces back together. Stifling. Despite the chill in the air, she stretched and pulled at her sweater collar.

"Are you too hot?" Carla rushed toward her waving a short stack of scratch paper. "We can open some of the doors and let a breeze through. Or I can make you a glass of lemonade."

"Let her make that lemonade." Tyrone called in from the bedroom. "She's an expert."

He had hovered over her throughout their cleaning job after Jay told him about her apartment. The bigmouth. Now the couple wouldn't let her breathe. Insisted on coming back here with her and cleaning up.

"You're sure Jay told you he swept this place?" How could he have? It was a wreck.

Tyrone moved to the doorframe. "I don't see how, but he checked prints, stains, did his imaging and photos, the works. Only found one set of prints besides yours, though."

"That one was probably Tasha's. She's here all the time." Was here. Dani sniffed and refused to dwell on her missing friend. Though at this point, the chances of any positive news seemed unlikely.

Her thoughts turned again to her other friends and extended family back home. Had they searched for her when she left? Did they wonder about her or worry? Not like she could do anything about it either way.

Carrying a box from her bedroom, Tyrone headed for the front door. "This is all destroyed, but I'm not tossing the photographs. I know a guy who knows a guy. I bet we can get those pics all stitched up for you."

If only. But she'd seen their state. If Dani's sewing on her couch wouldn't work, the shredded photos had no prayer. She folded the material over itself and pierced it with the needle. Good thing she'd given the ring to Jay. Whoever trashed her place had done a thorough search—had sifted through her salt and pepper shakers, dug into her half-gallon of Homemade Vanilla, and emptied every padded area in her home, including the kitchen stool and the rubber headrest in her bathtub.

With Carla's help, most of the re-stuffing and mending had been done. Tyrone avoided the needles but had set her kitchen back in order and dumped the items that hadn't survived. Then he started in on her bedroom.

Her friend knotted the thread on a seat cushion and checked her phone. "I have a Zumba class. You want to come?"

Dani laughed. "Oh, honey, I'd hate to hurt somebody with my lack of grace."

"I'd debate that with you, but I'm gonna be late. I'll bring taco salads when I come back."

"Thanks, sweetheart." Tyrone met her at the door and gave her a kiss.

"She doesn't have to bring dinner."

"Nonsense. What are friends for?" He returned to her bedroom as his phone rang.

Left alone with her thoughts, Dani tried to stay positive. But how could she? Tasha had been gone for four days already. No word besides the package. If someone had grabbed her because of the ring, he had no reason to keep her around now that Dani had the item.

And her apartment served as testimony; whoever he was knew that Dani had possession of the ring. If only she hadn't gone to that stupid pawn shop.

She picked up a ripped throw pillow. It wasn't worth trying to save. Shoving it into the kitchen trash can, she lifted the filled cylinder and made for the door.

"I'll take that." Tyrone came out of the bedroom, his lips pressed together and angling downward instead of curved in his usual smile.

"You know Jay would have my hide if I let you outta my sight before he got here."

"He's probably outside already."

He shook his head. "He called a couple of hours ago. I don't expect him until after Carla returns."

Tyrone took the can from her but set it down instead of going to empty it. He stared at the floor. A wrinkle formed between his eyebrows.

"Something's wrong. What have you heard?"

He closed his eyes for a second and rubbed the back of his neck with his hand. When he opened them again, he leveled an intense gaze at her. "Give me the ring, Dani."

Her spine iced. Jay hadn't told him anything about why her apartment had been trashed. They had agreed that the fewer people who knew about it, the better. "What are you talking about?"

"That's not gonna play." He put out his hand. "I've checked your purse, so the only place it could be is on you. Let's have it."

A slow burn started at the base of her neck. "You mean you did this? You trashed my place? You kidnapped Tasha?" She swung both fists at him, but he clamped his hands around her wrists.

Grime Beat

Chapter Twelve

"I need your help." Jay tracked his partner across the yard.

Cal laughed, flinging his hand outward. "And why should I help you?"

"Because a young woman's life is at stake. And another one is in danger."

"The brunette that came calling a couple of days ago?"

Jay nodded. He wanted to explain things further but needed his trust first. "I think…" Did he have any real reason to suspect, besides his gut? "I think Ethan might have something to do with a woman's disappearance."

His friend turned, eyes narrowed. He released an audible exhale. "Get in."

Jay shook his head. "Better take my car. Ethan's never seen it." Not to mention the hidden ring. Which he wouldn't.

"Fine." After Cal buckled up, he crossed his arms. "You gonna tell me what this is about?"

"Money." Jay focused on the road, but through his peripheral vision, took in Cal's every movement. Every breath, motion, vocal inflection, and body language. "For starters, how does an almost rookie officer like Ethan Hall afford a house in this classy neighborhood and an apartment downtown?"

"Good question. *I* can't even afford this neighborhood."

"Got an answer?" He pulled to a red light and turned toward his longtime mentor.

"Nope. And in answer to your next question, Miranda only knows how to spend money. She's not so good at making any." Cal's gaze was clear, his anger must've evaporated.

"I need to get into that downtown apartment."

"I can show it to you. Followed him out there one time for Miranda. She wanted pictures of his companion, but no woman ever showed." He turned his head toward Jay. "But you don't really think you're going to get a warrant to search a cop's place?" He snorted. "Based on what?"

"Missing items from the lock-up on his watch." Okay, only one item, but the gap in evidence trail added a separate issue. "And a woman who happened to recognize a piece of evidence that shouldn't have been at a pawn shop. A woman who has since disappeared."

Cal sobered and pulled out his phone. "Why didn't you tell me about this?"

Jay booted his mounted tablet to access the missing person's records, but the light turned green. "Get the record for Natasha Sanderson." He headed south, merging onto the interstate that would transport him to downtown.

His friend tapped on the screen. "Sanderson?"

"Yeah. Natasha, spelled like it sounds."

"No record of her. Not even an N. Sanderson."

"Try Tasha." Even though he knew it wouldn't be there.

Cal shook his head. "Huh-uh. Maybe they found her."

Not as of that morning when Jay had checked in at the department. "I put in the pictures myself. Something's off." Did Ethan Hall have access to delete missing-person's records? "Contact

Kirkland. He's the one who initiated the file." Messed up as it was.

Cal made the call, but Jay could tell from the one-sided conversation that the man had no idea about the file. Didn't even remember hearing about a missing girl named Natasha.

"Probably because he put her name in as Nancy." Jay had changed it when he put in the pictures, for the good that it did, now that the whole file had disappeared.

"If you're sure that girl is still gone, I think you might be right about someone on the force trying to cover something up." Cal speed-dialed and spoke to a local judge they both knew. After he hung up, he turned to Jay. "You have your warrant. But let me guess. You thought I might be mixed up in all of this."

"You taught me to think with my head and not my emotions. They're never right anyway. Isn't that what you said?"

"Poetically expressed with my recent doomed relationship." Cal leaned back in his seat.

Twenty minutes later, they stopped in a no parking zone. Jay left his grill lights strobing across the walls of a renovated factory and grabbed his crime scene bag as he got out.

Cal raised his eyes to the roof and back. "Studios. High dollar." He headed for an entrance displaying the management company's logo etched in gold.

Jay eyed the side of the building where smooth, gray metal created spacious patios against what looked like the original exterior. "1940s maybe?" He let his hand linger against the stone for a moment before pulling on one of the double glassed doors. "Nice place."

"You investigating or drooling over it?" Cal's brow ruffled. He stormed through the entrance with Jay in his wake. A calming waterfall that filled one wall had no effect on the man. He advanced toward a woman seated at a desk. "Are you the manager?"

"No. He's not available. Can I help you?" Her composure in the face of Cal's fuming was impressive.

His partner let his wallet drop open, exposing his badge. "I have a warrant for studio J. Open it."

She examined his badge. "Where's your warrant?"

Cal huffed. He unfolded the receipt-sized page from Jay's dashboard remote printer. "Signed by Judge Varnham."

"Hmm." She picked up a key ring and led them back outside, locking the office door behind her. "Studio J is at the end of this row, has a front entrance on the street and a side entrance by the alley, bedroom loft, kitchen. All the amenities." She paused at the last door.

"We're not in the market, lady." Cal pointed to the knob. "Just unlock it, please."

She rolled her eyes before turning her back. The lock clicked, and she faced them. "Will that be all?"

"We'll holler if we need anything else."

Her mouth curved into a momentary fake smile before she scampered back to her den.

Cal's head turned, following her departure. Really? Pretty females were as irresistible as cookies to Cal. "Didn't the last hour teach you anything?"

Cal scowled at him. "Old habits." He pushed the door open to reveal a huge space.

A huge empty space.

Jay tried to catch the receptionist, but she'd already entered the office. "Is this where Ethan's living?"

"Doesn't look like anyone lives here." Their voices echoed off bare walls, to the thirty-foot ceiling and back. Jay peered into what must have been a kitchen at some point. As empty as the rest of the apartment.

Cal trotted up the steps to a landing. "Something's up there."

Jay followed. A large loft created a ceiling for the kitchen and hung over roughly half of the wide space on the first floor. Pizza boxes and beer cans littered the carpet surrounding a black recliner. A flat-screen TV hung on the wall with a mini-fridge below it.

Cal opened the door. "Baloney and beer."

"This is weird. All this space."

"And this exclusive address." Cal shook his head. "I don't get it. Hall doesn't seem the type to live in a place like this."

He wasn't society. But the clutter didn't fit either. "I don't think he even eats pizza. He always wants sushi." Jay picked through the minimal trash in an attempt to find anything resembling evidence. Finding nothing, he and Cal swept the corners of the bottom floor.

"Zilch." Cal stood in the center of the room and scanned the walls. "Not a clue in sight."

Jay stared at the plush carpeting. "Unless you look down." He pointed out deep indentations in the rug. "Something heavy."

Cal took a few steps toward the outside wall. "Some things."

"Furniture?" Maybe from a former tenant? Though the marks didn't look like they were made by furniture.

His partner was on his knees near the alley-side wall. "Carpet's been pulled up over here. Laid back in place."

Why? Jay fingered some residue embedded in the thick rug.

Cal knocked on the brick. "There's a way in over here. I'm sure of it." He continued his tapping along the perimeter.

"Probably used to be. It was a warehouse."

He rubbed the sand-like substance between his fingers and smelled it. Sawdust? Or something like it.

Cal's tap suddenly took on the twang of metal. He flicked what looked like a mood-lighting fader switch, and a large section of the wall moved upward, the track camouflaged with paint that imitated the mottled brick of the historic building. "He was storing something here."

Electricity erupted down Jay's spine. "That's exactly what he's doing." He held his fingers out

to Cal. "I bet he had crates in here at one time."
He pulled a baggie from his black satchel and
brushed the light-colored powder into the plastic
container. "He only stays here once in a while,
right?" He pulled out his phone and flicked
pictures of the open wall, the carpet indentations,
and the embedded dust.

"According to Miranda." Cal hit the button to
lower the make-shift door back into place. "Never
the same days of the week, though."

They walked back to the office. Jay stepped
inside and lifted his hand. "We're finished with
Studio J. You can lock it back up, now."

The woman pasted a fake smile in place.
"Thank you so much."

Cal had followed him. He leaned over the
counter, doing his traditional intimidator spiel, not
that it would work with this woman. "Do I need to
tell you that this visit isn't for discussion?
Especially not with Ethan Hall."

Her mocking smirk dropped off. "Who's he?"

"The guy who's leasing that studio apartment.
It is Ethan Hall, right?"

"Hmm." She tapped on her computer. "Studio
J... that unit... is leased by a Ryan Kirkland."

Dani struggled against the grip Tyrone had on her. "You jerk. What have you done with Tasha?"

"Settle down, girl. I didn't have anything to do with Tasha, or your apartment." She stopped struggling, and he loosened his hold. "But Tasha is in trouble. You know that. I just got a call from a guy. If you'll turn over the ring, he'll let her go."

She pulled away from him. "That's crazy." She bolted for the door and yanked it open. The doorknob slipped from her grasp as Dani plowed headfirst into the uniformed policeman standing there. He shoved her back and pulled out a weapon with a silencer. Dani stumbled over Jay's blanket and fell on her behind.

Tyrone stepped between her and the officer. "No need for that. She's getting the ring. All we want is for Tasha to come back."

The man shoved the door shut. "Took too long." His voice sounded more like an angry animal than a human being.

"She just needs to fetch it. Dani, give the ring to the man."

Scooting backward, she halted when she hit the end-table next to the couch. Something rocked and fell. She watched the cop. His dead eyes pierced Tyrone. He wasn't going to let Tasha go. None of them would walk away from this. She wrapped her hand around cold metal. Sturdy. Must've knocked over one of the candlesticks.

The cop shifted his gaze. "Where is the ring?"

She shook her head. "I don't have it anymore."

"Listen…." Tyrone lifted his hand. "We can work this all out. If you'll—"

The growl turned to rage, and he practically threw Tyrone against the wall.

Dani scrambled to her feet with the candlestick. The gun discharged with a pump that jarred the air. Tyrone cried out.

"Don't lie to me." He advanced on her.

"I'm not," she shouted. She pressed her back to the wall. "You know it isn't here."

He braced his forearm against her collarbone. "Where, then?" A younger man than she first thought, his sleeve smelled of fish. He kept looking over his shoulder at Tyrone. If only she had a good angle, she'd conk him a good one while his face was turned. But it wouldn't likely knock him out. Not from this close.

"I hid it at my work." She kept her voice

steady and her eyes trained on him. "At the Kellerman warehouse." Not a flinch or regret over her bald-faced lie.

"The man over there is dead if you're lying." He pushed away from her.

Tyrone lay sprawled, his leg bleeding. Dani rushed to him and snatched up Jay's blanket to act as a temporary bandage. He groaned and tried to sit up.

"Hold this in place." She put his hand over the blanket. When she stood, she kept the heavy brass piece hidden behind her baggy jeans.

"Tell me where the ring is." He aimed the gun at Tyrone's head, but the twitch in his eye revealed his character. This man was no killer. Not yet, anyway.

"How do I know you'll let him live? How do I know you'll let either of us live?"

"Wrong answer." He pointed the gun at her.

Peace enveloped her. Real peace. And calm. "Well, you won't get your ring back that way." She turned to her right and moved to the end table, setting up a fallen lamp with her empty hand. "I want to live, and I want my friend to live, but I'm not afraid of death. Not nearly as afraid as you are." She turned back to face him. At this angle, she'd be able to deliver a solid hit.

"Stop talking. Tell me where the ring is." His gaze faltered.

"Oh, dear, you'll never find it at the warehouse by yourself. Seriously. Your little ring won't be found for years, if ever." She lifted her chin. "If you let us go, you'll be safe. Nothing can prove that you stole evidence or pawned it at the shop."

"You want to see your friend die?" He pointed the gun at Tyrone again.

"No, I don't. Because if something were to happen to him or to me, our company would have to do an intensive inventory. I bet they'd find that ring and the rest of the evidence against you in less than a half-hour. How long would it take professionals to figure out what you've done? It only took Tasha a weekend." She hoped there was enough truth in there to convince him.

His mouth twitched. "Think you're so smart."

She shook her head. "If I had been smart, I'd have realized that only some officer from the evidence lock-up could have stolen the ring. Instead, I let my emotions get away from me, thinking Jay Hunter had a part in the theft." If only the man would look at Tyrone again.

He scoffed. "Hunter don't know his right hand from his left."

At least Jay knew proper grammar. She needed a diversion to get him to stop staring at her. "Maybe not, but he's narrowing down his people of interest. Does he consider you a suspect yet?"

His eyes hardened.

Maybe Tyrone would see what she was attempting? How could she encourage him into action?

"We're going to check out that warehouse together." The cop reached for her shoulder.

The wrong side. Even if he did look away, she had no angle. Her final chance slipped away.

Chapter Thirteen

Kirkland? Really? Jay nosed his sedan northward. With what they found in the downtown studio, they decided to check out his apartment in one of the nearby suburbs.

Cal leaned an arm on the ledge of the passenger window. "Hard to imagine that aging, dumpy guy with the style and intelligence of a middle-schooler living in such a posh residence."

Not exactly the way Jay would've said it, but close. "It's clear he's been housing something in that bottom floor."

Cal shrugged. "Coulda been Christmas presents for all we know."

Hopefully, the fifty-year-old apartments he parked in front of would hold more promise. This place made better sense for a guy like Kirkland anyway. No family to speak of, besides an ex-wife. Never moved up from an entry level position in all his years on the force. Though, as to that, Jay could hardly judge the man.

"No receptionist here." Cal chuckled as he knocked on a dilapidated door labeled Manager.

Jay eyed the bare lot that served as a yard. Dirt instead of grass. Dead bushes surrounded the tan-brick building. Cracked sidewalks continued a broken line that tracked the grout all the way across the wall.

Cal knocked again, pounding this time.

A boy, ten at the most, opened the door. He was dressed in faded flannel and holey jeans. "My dad's sleeping."

"Shouldn't you be in school?"

The kid lowered his chin. "You want something, mister?"

Cal showed his badge. The kid backed up so fast he bumped into the wall behind him. "I dint know what they was doing."

Jay's ears perked up. He pushed the door wider. A snore erupted from some interior room. Jay knelt in front of the boy. "What who was doing?" He practically whispered to keep dad asleep.

"Those men with that girl. They tell me to mind my business, but I heared her crying." The boy wiped his nose. "You're not gonna arrest me, are you?"

"Your dad know about the girl?" Cal laid a hand on the kid's shoulder.

He shook his head. "I don't think he's heard her. He's been working double shifts."

"Show me where she is." Could this be Tasha? Or was some other poor woman in trouble?

The kid tiptoed into the next room and came out with a ring of keys. He led them up the stairs to the apartment directly overhead. "She was crying a little while ago."

After he unlocked the door, Jay pushed him aside. "Go back downstairs and wait inside with your dad. Don't come out until I say so."

He put his hand on the knob and withdrew his weapon from the holster under his jacket. Cal matched his pose as they both watched the kid descend. As soon as the downstairs door closed Jay eased against the one in front of him to edge it open a crack. A wave of pollutants hit his nose. Compost, rotting food, but nothing smelled dead.

That was good. "Police. We have a warrant."

"Here. I'm in here." A frantic female voice rose from the back bedroom.

Jay squared against the wall and eyed the clutter. Every flat space held empty dishes, pizza boxes, fast food bags, and a variety of trashy movies if the covers could be believed. He slid right and let his partner inside. No movement, no other noise. He passed a cracked tile floor that marked where a kitchen should be, under piles of trash.

He and Cal met across the room, at a closed door. The female continued to shout, though her husky voice indicated she'd tried that for long periods before. How could no one else have heard her? More than likely they'd ignored her.

Cal nodded and pushed the door open. Jay leaped inside with gun pointed.

"Don't shoot. Don't shoot me." Tasha, chained by one wrist to the frame of a huge iron bed, held both hands in front of her.

"You're Tasha Sanderson, right?" Jay holstered his gun and took the woman's shackled hand. Swollen from obvious attempts to escape and streaked with dried blood, it needed medical care. They had to figure out some way to release her.

"You're that cop from the crime scenes."

Jay gave a half smile. "Dani's been worried about you."

Cal had completed surveillance of the closet and bathroom. "I'll call this in."

Jay put a hand on his shoulder. "Not a good idea, if Kirkland or Hall are in on this."

"A cop hauled me in here. Arrested me for some bogus charge and then locked me up in here. I don't know his name, though." Tasha shoved her greasy, blonde curls out of her face.

"We need to get her out of here." Cal pulled out his phone. "Got an idea."

While Cal worked on his plan, Jay jotted notes from Tasha. The ring, the pawn shop, and a description of the big brute that tossed her in here. "The guy at the shop showed me all sorts of things that came in at the same time as the ring I found. Jewelry, electronics, guns. Like there had been a shipment or something."

Or an unloaded storage unit. He looked at Cal as he pocketed his phone. "How much you want to bet that the shop where she found the missing evidence was raided not too long ago."

"Would be brilliant. Timing the movement of

stolen goods until after the theft squad raided the local fences." Cal shook his head. "More brains than I'd have given Kirkland credit for."

Jay talked more with Tasha, checking for indications of further injuries, abuse, or drugging. She seemed to be in fairly good health. "The guy would bring me a sandwich every morning. And I had water from the bathroom."

At least her chain gave her enough freedom to go that far, though it wouldn't reach to the window on the other side of the room or the little one in the bathroom.

In what felt like minutes, Cal's phone call contact walked in with a blow torch and a patch on his mechanic shirt that read Bubba. His black eyes hardened when he caught sight of Tasha. "I don't cotton to tying up ladies." He shoved his mask into place and lit the flame.

"Don't touch anything that you don't have to." Cal pointed toward the wrought iron that held the padlock.

"Gotcha." The man tightened the flame and cut through the chain.

Cal shook his hand. "I knew you were the man to call. Keep this quiet until we can take care of the ones who did this." He pulled the broken link through the handcuff attached to Tasha's wrist.

"Count on it." Bubba returned to the door.

Jay held up his hand urging him to pause. He checked the lot and surrounding area for signs of Kirkland. Nothing. He led them down the steps, then separated when they headed for the cars.

Clouds began to fill in where the blue sky had been. A cold wind kicked up as Jay tapped on the manager's door. The kid poked his head out like he'd been standing there the whole time. "Is the lady okay, mister?"

Jay nodded and ruffled the boy's curly hair. "You did good, kid." He handed him his business card. "Don't be afraid to call me if you ever need help again."

Cal had his phone out again by the time Jay returned to the car. "We're taking the woman to the ER to get the shackle removed." He mouthed Lieutenant Gates's name. Their supervisor knew how to proceed with this matter.

Jay eyed her in his rear-view mirror. "You all right?" He steered his car toward the closest Emergency room.

She nodded. "Thankful to be outta there."

"Well, we're gonna get you checked out all

the same." Cal pointed out the hospital on the right. "Gates is meeting us. I'll catch a ride back to the station."

Good. Maybe after he checked in with Dani and Tyrone, he and Cal could decide how to approach Kirkland.

"How are you gonna get the guy? I mean, he's a cop, right?" Except for her wrist, Tasha hadn't shown any other injuries. And her spunky voice made her sound no worse for the wear.

"Working on it." He pulled under the covered drive and let her and Cal out. Knowing who was behind all of this didn't solve the problem. They needed a fast plan to catch this guy. Before the man found out his captive had escaped.

And that she had help.

Dani stared at the cop. "I'll need my purse if I'm supposed to get us into the warehouse."

He let go of her shoulder and backed up a step. "Where?"

If only he would look away. She pressed the solid brass to the back of her leg. "I think in that chair." She pointed with her empty hand.

Still, he didn't move. Infuriating.

At that moment, someone pounded at the front door. "It's me," Jay shouted.

The cop spun toward the door. Dani leapt forward, bringing the candlestick down on his head as hard as she could. He screamed and cursed. The door flew open, and another group of muffled shots erupted from the gun.

Dani didn't wait to see where they hit. She dashed to the bedroom. She flung open the sliding glass door and looked over the rail. Maybe she could climb to the lower apartment. But hers wasn't set up as easy a climb as Tasha's had been.

"Come back here." The cop spewed expletives in a slurring voice.

She hopped onto the banister and wobbled. She grabbed the roof to balance. Nothing to brace against. The ground teased her from way too far beneath her tennis shoes. Going down was no option.

The man inside bellowed something indistinguishable. Ice crawled up her spine. No time to make a plan. She pivoted on the narrow beam. Wind blew straight into her face as she glanced over the eave. A higher stretch than she'd had the last time, but there was a slight angle, gable-like that she could use.

A crash sounded from the living room. Maybe her strike had made him lose balance? She wasn't about to go back and find out. She braced her palms on the rooftop. It jutted out too far, but she had no choice. She leaped and swung her feet to the right, reaching for the gutter attached to the corner. One foot caught, and she did a mid-air push up and pulled her other foot to the side of her hands, elephant walking up the steep slope.

The January that couldn't make up its mind switched on again. The warm, spring-like day turned frigid. Her plaid shirt and hair whipped around as gray clouds scuttled overhead.

What had happened to Jay? The thought tormented her, but she couldn't allow worry to steal her brief head-start.

She attempted to climb the incline, but a few steps from the edge, her foot slipped. The shingles had little, if any, traction. She belly-crawled to the gable that covered her porch and paused for a breath.

The cop clomped out onto the wood planks of her small patio, directly beneath her. He muttered. "What'd you do, sprout wings, girl?" Obviously not in his right mind.

"Where are you?" His voice exploded. Her neighbors had to hear that. Surely someone would call the police.

She hoped that was the wisest course of action, considering that one of their own was trying to kill her.

God, please let Jay and Tyrone be all right. And Carla. She was due back soon. What a failure. Dani had left her friends in the apartment with that madman. Shifting, she glanced at the highest point of the roof behind her. It sloped on the other side to the stairs and front entry. That would be an easier dismount than trying to climb to the ground. And she'd be on the exit side of the apartment.

Something bumped over the track of the sliding door. "I know you're up there, Dani. Kirkland told me about how you didn't know how to climb down."

Any second, she'd see his ugly face breech the edge of the roof. Or worse, the gun. Over the top was her only chance. Once again flattening against the roof, she shuffled upward as fast as the slick shingles allowed.

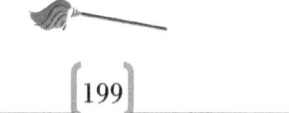

Jay's only thought had been anticipation for the joy in Dani's eyes when he told her that Tasha was okay. The man's scream had jolted him. The stream of expletives and threats moved him to action. He slammed his foot just under the knob with all the thrust he could offer. Wood splintered. Muffled shots sounded as he shoved against the barrier once more.

But his entrance had halted at that point. A burn ricocheted through his body and caused him to stumble. His vision spiraled. Then, he tasted carpet threads. Wait, how long had he been on the floor? Had someone hit him? He tried to push up but cutting pain deep in his left shoulder halted his motion.

I've been shot?

"You okay?" Tyrone's words came in a grunt more than a voice.

Jay rolled over and pushed up with his other hand. He looked for his gun. "I'm alive. For now." Rivulets of blood darkened his navy dress shirt. "And you?"

"He got my leg. Some cop."

And he was after Dani. But Jay was in no position to help her. Not without a weapon. He didn't even know where she'd gone. He braced himself to stand against the broken frame. Then he tipped a stool over and shoved it against the door to keep it open.

The shooter had disappeared, probably into Dani's bedroom or the porch beyond. His voice still carried, though Jay couldn't make out his words. He slipped out the front door and went down on a knee. If nothing else, he'd have the element of surprise. He pulled out his phone and dialed Cal.

"Hey, ugly. Your friend is going to be all right."

"Good to know." Jay lowered his voice as something clattered in the back room and the shooter yelled something else. At least as long as he yelled, he didn't likely have Dani in sight. "I think I've found Ethan Hall."

"Where are you?"

He gave the address. "Sounds like Hall, though I haven't had a good look at him." He took a deep breath and glanced at the growing stain on his sleeve. "And send paramedics. I've been shot."

That would get Cal moving in double-time. He disconnected and laid his phone beside him. A blue plaid tennis shoe bobbed over the edge of the roof not far from his spot.

Directly above the stairs. Bad placement. "Further right. Three feet right." His forceful whisper wasn't loud enough to be heard by whoever raised a ruckus at the back of the apartment.

The foot disappeared then reappeared over a solid ledge.

"Yes."

The shoe rolled over and was joined by another before Dani's blue-jean-clad legs appeared. They dangled for a moment, then one toe touched the metal rail beneath her. She got her balance and hopped to the cement floor.

Her eyes lit as they met his, but thundering feet from inside the apartment alerted him. While Dani darted around a corner, Jay prepared to tackle the charging rhino.

Chapter Fourteen

Dani prickled at the warning in Jay's eyes. She scampered into the opposite corner of the deck, only somewhat hidden from her doorway.

Jay's muscles tensed, and he flung himself at the cop when the big man lumbered outside. The guy hit the rail and smacked his head against the wall. His gun fell out of his hand, and Dani dashed for it.

The cop, younger by a couple of years than Jay, recovered from the hit on his head quickly enough. He reared back and let loose a powerful swing.

Jay ducked and dropped to one knee. She got her first good look at the man attempting to be her hero. Blood stained one side of his dress shirt. Her stomach flipped.

The cop stretched to slam his fists against the back of Jay's neck.

"That's enough." Dani squared and pointed the silenced weapon at his face. "I might not be practiced at firing this thing, but I guarantee I can do some damage from this short distance."

The cop lifted his hands. "Aren't you the superhero?"

Jay leaned back against the wall and used it to push into a standing posistion as another cop ascended the stairs with his gun drawn.

Pointed at her. "Young lady, put down your weapon."

A shiver crawled across her shoulders. The barrel of that gun would haunt her dreams for years. She recognized the man, Kirkland, from the last time she'd had a climb over the roof. Was this guy the cavalry at last?

The guarded look from Jay told her no. "How many men are here with you, Kirkland?"

His face transformed into plain meanness. "What are you doing here, Hunter? A simple disturbing the peace isn't normally your beat."

"Nothing simple about this," Jay said. "We found Tasha."

Dani's eyes widened. They found her? Or they found her body? Her insides knotted, but she kept the gun raised, training it on the officer slowly ascending the stairs.

"You're putting me in a predicament, Hunter." Kirkland kept his eyes on her. "Seems we have a woman here who shot one police officer and threatened another."

"Not gonna fly, man. Cal's already made the report. They're looking for you. Both of you."

Kirkland twitched. A wicked smile spread across his face. "A bluff? Really, Jay? You won't even play poker with us, but you'll try a juvenile ploy like that one?"

The big cop grunted. "I'm not up for any killing. You said no one would get hurt."

"You want to go to jail?" Kirkland stopped at the top step.

"Don't listen to him, Ethan." Jay groaned as he leaned heavily into the wall. "You're both going to jail. But you don't have to go for murder."

Dani kept her eyes trained on the other cop's hand, but alarms went off in her head over Jay's weakening state and obvious pain.

"I didn't murder nobody. All I did was store

the hot stuff and keep an ear out for the raids."

"Shut up, idiot." Kirkland's growl dwindled as red and blue lights flickered across the parking lot.

"Why?" Jay smirked. "Seems clear enough. You two stored stolen goods and then had them moved to prime fences after the raids. Smart."

"Smarter than you, living your daddy's dream and trying to be somebody. All you get is a commemorative plaque and a pat on the back." He snorted. "Not for me. I have quite a retirement."

She stared at the empty, old man over the sight of the other guy's gun. What a pathetic state.

"Put down your weapon, Officer Kirkland." Someone had a bullhorn.

He flinched. His reverie must have camouflaged the arrival of legitimate officers. The cop tilted his chin without taking his eyes off her. "I have an armed suspect and an injured man."

Footsteps sounded on the stairs beneath them. The bullhorn buzzed. "We know about the injured officer. And the missing woman… everything."

Kirkland's eyes pierced her for a moment, but she stared back at him. Her right ankle began to quiver.

Dropping his gaze, he lowered his weapon.

Jay pushed away from the wall and grabbed the gun from his hand. "I'm lousy at poker. Can't bluff to save my life."

Dani set the silenced gun down and raised her hands as several officers arrived. "I have another injured friend in there." One went through her door while the others escorted the two dirty members of their team down the steps.

She darted to Jay as he sagged against the wall. "Let me help you sit." With his good arm about her shoulders, she lowered him to the cold floor of the deck.

"I'm okay." He caught her eyes. "Good job, Watson."

She smiled but backed away as three emergency workers surrounded him.

She followed one of the EMTs to her doorway. Tyrone blinked at her from in front of the couch. "I'm fine, Dani. Just hurting." He grunted. "Glad I helped you clean all this up before he took out my knee."

A paramedic joined the EMTs. As one attached Tyrone to a bag of liquids, the medic scanned the wound. "A doctor won't know for sure until he removes the bullet, but from the looks of the wound, I think your knee will recover."

"And Jay?" Dani's voice broke. "The injured officer outside?"

"Funny thing that." The paramedic continued quick work on Tyrone as he spoke. "I guess the bullet is lodged in there in such a way as to cut off the bleeding. He sure should have lost more blood than he has." He smiled. "I think he'll be fine."

Well done, Sherlock. She let the men work as she wandered back onto the second-floor deck. The EMTs had moved Jay onto a stretcher, his face pale under his dark hair. An oxygen mask covered his mouth, and his eyes remained closed.

Tears moistened her lashes. She'd brought him to this. Her intense need to investigate. And for what?

A man in a blazer and tie crossed toward her as Jay was taken down the stairs. "Miss Foster? I'm Officer Cutter, Jay's partner."

"Yes?" She kept her focus on Jay's dark head as it descended.

"He asked me to tell you that your friend, Natasha, is going to be fine."

Lifting the last box out of her car trunk, Dani shut the lid and paused for a moment, getting her balance as she propped up the container on the Honda. She eyed the new place. Comparable to the old one, again on the second floor with three sides of windows, but rough pine siding gave off a lovely smell with every trip up the stairs.

This place had a security fence around it, too. Something Matthew had insisted upon when he learned of her situation, after he'd finished chewing her out for not contacting him about the break-in. Arguing back did no good. But she wrote up a little report about the entire experience, including her call to him when she'd been shot at by Ethan Hall. If nothing else, the Marshall's Office would have a record of her side of the story.

She picked up the box and climbed the outer stairs. The place looked safer than her last one. And it was more expensive, but at least that part of the problem was somewhat taken care of.

The box bumped into the facing of the door as she tried to maneuver through the frame. "I think this is the last of it."

"Let me help you." Carla guided the bulky load through the doorway. "Don't you love the smell of a new place?"

Not so much, but the thought of permanently returning to her old apartment sickened her. Even after almost two weeks of bunking in the back room at the Reids' house. She smiled and nodded. "I can't thank you two enough for letting me hang with you."

"Honey, you were more than welcome. You didn't have to leave, either."

But the timing had been right. Easy enough to break her contract after the break-in. And she'd have to move anyway while the complex finally got around to cleaning things up. Just as well to move a bit closer to Tyrone and Carla. Closer to Jay, too, according to him, but she wouldn't let that enter into her thoughts.

Jay and Tyrone shouted at some great basketball play on the TV and fist-bumped. Jay lounged on the couch with his arm in a sling. Tyrone, his knee in a brace, commandeered the recliner that Tasha had contributed to their apartment.

Her blonde friend exited the kitchen with a crockpot full of chili con queso. "Anyone hungry?"

Both men raised their hands.

Dani had experienced a bit of trepidation about rooming with Tasha. Bringing her into potential peril if only by sheer proximity. But after all she'd been through already, this situation couldn't be much more dangerous. And her roommate hadn't been any more interested in living alone again than Dani was.

"How's your Aunt Dodie?" While Dani stayed with the Reids to catch her breath, Tasha had spent the week at the home of her aunt about seventy-five miles south of Fort Worth.

"Doing well. She came to the farm with me while I was there. Her hip has healed as well as it's going to, but thankfully, she likes the center. She'd never be able to take care of the farm now that she has to use a walker." Her friend returned to the kitchen and Dani followed.

"I'm glad she joined me. Living at her place, up in the boonies with nothing except a neighbor a half-mile away…" She emptied a bag of tortilla chips into a bowl. "It was nice to recuperate after the hospital released me, but I'm a city girl. That much quiet with no one else around would keep me awake at night."

Dani could relate.

"Besides, I can keep visiting Aunt Dodie on

the weekends, but I really need to keep my weekday job."

"Have you spoken to Mr. Kellerman?" Dani popped a chip in her mouth. She didn't mention how Frank had already declared her fired.

She smiled. "He was so nice. Gave me the last two weeks and even argued with me when I told him I could start back on Monday. But I know with Tyrone out of commission you all have to be hurting for help."

That was putting it lightly. Dani and Frank did the last job by themselves. More like Frank pointed out things to clean while he played some stupid game on his smart phone. "We are, at that. Frank isn't exactly enthusiastic about continuing to fill in for Tyrone for the next couple of weeks." She followed Tasha back into the living room. The men dove into the cheese dip the moment the bowl of chips hit the coffee table.

"Won't be that long." Tyrone ate a chip and spoke through the crumbs. "Doc says I can probably start back next week sometime. No lifting, but after a couple more therapy sessions, I'll be good to go."

Excellent news. Dani had no trouble hauling out the heavy stuff if only to see less of Frank's smug, pointy face. "Here's to great therapy sessions." She dunked a chip in the dip and held it up.

"Hear, hear." The others followed suit. Dani crunched the chip. Spicy, but nothing compared to her last encounter with chips and dip.

They feasted and watched until the dip disappeared. Dani carried the crock pot back to the kitchen where Carla was rinsing cups and bowls.

"You don't have to do that." She set the heavy appliance on the counter next to the sink.

The slender woman assembled dishes in the washer. "Habit. I like moving around." Her light-brown curls tossed over her milk chocolate face as she bent forward.

Dani leaned against the counter. "So how is Tyrone really?" She'd made a point to stick to the little guest room when she was staying with them, to let them have their space. But when she did see him, all he did was smile and claim, "It's all good." The man tried to paint things rosier than they were.

"Smarting because he believes he's responsible for Jay's injury."

"That's ridiculous. Why would he think that?" And how could she live with him for two weeks and not have a hint of his unreasonable guilt?

She stood, bringing her lively curls back into place. "A cop, I guess that Ethan Hall fellow, called Tyrone. He inferred that you had stolen something, and kidnappers grabbed Tasha to force you to return it."

"He really thought I stole something?" Her heart ached.

"It all happened so fast that he didn't have time to think. The officer on the phone said you were responsible for holding on to a ransom that could save your friend's life."

Dani stared at the dull silver sink. Tyrone believed her to be that selfish and heartless? How had he hidden that for two weeks?

"All the man really wanted was to know where you were." She shook her head. "You have to know, honey. Tyrone feels terrible that the idea ever entered his head. He'd throw a fit if he knew I was telling you this. The cop put on the pressure. He said that you had been hiding. Tyrone let that detail slip out, then tried to fix things by getting the ring from you to keep you out of trouble."

"I guess I understand." And the description fit the timetable of what happened in her apartment.

"He's kicking himself for being taken in like

that."

"But the man was a policeman. I get it." And once the pain stopped, she probably would. "How about his injury?"

"Doing well. The doctor said that his recovery was remarkable."

"Good to hear." Dani pulled the liner from the crockpot and tossed the dirty plastic into the trash. She lowered the appliance to the floor and shoved it into a cabinet, willing the heat in her cheeks to cool. How could she face her friend again?

"Girl, you are my kind of cleaner. Wish they made things like that for frying pans and skillets." Carla laughed. "So... how are you and Jay getting along?"

From one uncomfortable subject to another. She'd sidestepped this conversation the entire time she'd been at the Reid's. Another reason why she had stuck to her own private quarters when she was in their home. "I wish you wouldn't get all worked up about that. He helped me. It's what police officers do."

"The good ones." Carla clicked her tongue against her teeth.

"That's most of them."

She shrugged. "Well, Jay's sure one of the

good ones."

Dani shook her head. "There's nothing between us."

Not even the dinner invitation they had shared. Of course, with the injuries of both men, the whole evening had been cancelled. But the likelihood of a raincheck became slimmer with each passing day. "And I don't expect there to be."

"Don't expect what?" Jay sauntered in and set his empty glass in the sink.

Carla's eyes flicked in her direction.

She couldn't lie. But misdirection had become second nature. "What do you think? Will we have any more winter after this warmup or are we done?"

Her friend rolled her eyes. Jay chuckled. "Never count on the weather around here."

Creaking and a thump from the other room declared the recliner righted. "Time to go, Carla."

"Ah, the bellow." She turned her dark eyes on Jay. "I assume the game is over?"

Jay smiled.

"And Tyrone's team lost. I can always tell by the bear's growl." She draped the towel on the oven handle. "Coming."

Dani and Jay followed her into the living room.

"I'll help you all out." Tasha grabbed one arm while Carla took the other. Dani said goodbye at the door and started back toward the kitchen when Jay stopped her.

He lifted a flat package from behind the couch. Not very big and wrapped in blue, plaid paper just like her tennis shoes.

"You didn't have to bring gifts. This is no housewarming."

He laughed. "No, it was a moving party, and all I did was sit on your couch and eat your food."

"Not like you could do much more than that with the horrible sling on your arm and stitches in your shoulder." She tore the paper off one side.

"It's really not that big a deal." He strolled toward the front door.

A wooden frame appeared. She turned it over and gasped. Her dad. The shredded picture. But it was perfect. Tears skewed her vision. "How did you…" She hugged the frame.

"I know a guy." He smiled and winked.

"It's…" Her voice broke. Holding the frame in one arm, she threw her other one around his neck. "Thank you." A whisper was the best she could muster.

"Guess he's a pretty special man." He returned a one-armed embrace.

Releasing him, her focus moved back to the picture. "My dad."

Jay stood close, his arm still around her waist.

How she wanted to share all of the horrible history. But for now, the secrecy still kept her safe. "Having this picture back means so much to me."

"I'm glad to do it." He started to move away, then closed in on her again. His eyes locked with hers. "How much?"

"Huh?" Did he want reimbursement or something? "I can write you a check."

He shut his eyes and shook his head. "I'm lousy at this."

"At what?"

When he opened his eyes, he sought hers again. "I'd like to spend some time with you. The two of us. Maybe dinner?"

"A date?" The concept floored her. She'd thoroughly succeeded in believing he had only helped her because it was his job.

"Yes, a date. Can I call you?" His half smile sent electric bolts clear to her toes.

Too flustered to answer, she nodded, feeling like a teenager.

He swung out of the door and glanced back. "See you around, Watson."

She watched him join the others at the parking lot. *You got that right, Sherlock.*

Grime Beat

Chapter One of Grime Wave
(Book #2)

"I didn't giggle." Dani Foster shouldered her purse while her friend fussed with the key in the office door.

"Yes, you did." Carla retracted the bolt and let Dani inside first. "Sounded just like a teenager heading for prom."

Stuff and nonsense. She made for the bathroom. "I only said my hair could use a little help after being stuck in the helmet all day." She pushed open the door. "Don't you want to primp?"

Carla let out a trill of laughter. Now *that* was a giggle. "I married my man. Don't have to impress him anymore." She laughed again and headed for the entrance next to a marble-topped counter in front of a stone facade. "I'll get my phone and meet you back here."

Her phone. The excuse to come by her office, but it was more likely Carla's attempt to calm Dani's nerves about this first official date with Jay. She stared at the mirror and fluffed her hair.

It had taken long enough to get to this point. February was a brutal month for suicides. Her dad had taught her that. If Jay's schedule had been anything like hers, he'd barely had time for a shower.

She applied a little lipstick and brushed on gloss over it. Too much. Made her look like an adolescent in addition to simply sounding like one. A paper towel dispensed with the gloss. She touched up the color and surveyed herself. Not too bad. Her makeup had held. No stray mascara. Her long hair still had some curl to the bangs, waves and body throughout.

Tucking a stray strand behind her ear, she spritzed some perfume, shoved it and her lipstick back inside her purse, then pulled open the door. "I'm ready as I'll ever be." A curl of anticipation crawled through her insides. Nerves. Good grief. Now she *felt* like a kid.

"Carla, did you find your phone?" She paused at the opening and listened for a response. Nothing.

"We don't want to be too late." A lousy way to start any date, but especially a first one, and after over a month of trying to fit it in.

She walked down a makeshift hallway with a wall on her left and a cubicle matrix on her right. "Are you still back here?" She glanced into the first cube. One bare desk and the other cluttered with photos and children's art along with notepads, empty file folders, and an *I Love My*

Mama coffee mug.

The silence of the empty room flinched when a noisy heater kicked on. The back of Dani's neck prickled. "Carla?" Her voice took on a soft, squeaky texture. Where was that woman?

The last time Dani had worried about a friend, her roommate Tasha had been kidnapped. But such couldn't be the case this time. Dani had only been in the bathroom ten minutes, max.

A muffled sound came from behind her, farther into the maze. Hard to say if it was a cry or an answer. Dani moved in that direction and started to call again but halted. Being a detective's daughter brought the caution out in her. Why advertise where she was? Especially if there was a reason for the knot tightening around her middle.

She peeked into the next cube on her right but saw no one and took another step. *Wait a minute.* She poked her head back around the opening.

A tiny rivulet of reddish-brown seeped under the gap of the false wall opposite her. Blood?

"Carla!" With both hands, she pushed against the edge of the wall and propelled herself around the corner to where the liquid had to originate.

Her friend knelt, rather bowed, barely inside the entrance. Dani gasped and dropped to her knees behind her. "Are you hurt?" Her back and head didn't show signs of blood. "*Where* are you hurt? How?" Images from her horror almost a year ago—almost a life ago—flooded her mind.

Her stomach recoiled at the vision and her muscles stiffened for a second.

But that had been a hopeless situation last summer. Well before her arrival in Dallas. And it had nothing to do with her friend.

Carla was still breathing. Still upright. Dani braced her friend's shoulder with one hand and felt for a pulse on her neck.

Then she saw the source of the blood.

Look for GRIME WAVE at Amazon.

For Discussion & Study

1. As the story opens, Dani is desperate to find some hint of where her friend, Tasha, has gone. I'm reminded of the truth in Proverbs 18:24. I bet you can think of specific people who have shown this type of loyalty in your life. What are some things they have done to gain them this honored opinion?

2. What are some actions you've taken that prove your commitment or dedication to a friend?

3. In most translations of this verse, it notes that there is "a" friend who sticks closer than a brother. John 15:14-15 gives more insight on this. How have you seen this relationship in your own life?

4. Dani has trouble trusting the police. She feels, especially after discovering the source of the item she received in her package, that someone near Jay, if not Jay himself, isn't honest. What makes trust such an integral part in any relationship?

5. Micah 7:1-7 speaks to the subject of trust rather negatively. But realistically, anyone can betray. Have you ever been the victim of betrayal? Have you ever been the perpetrator of one? What initiated the treachery and what was the result? How did the relationship survive, if it did?

6. Dani and Jay have a discussion about trust.

> Dani lowered her chin. "People are people, whether cops, clergy, or businessmen. They don't become all-perfect superheroes just because they take on a job."
>
> "You sound a little cynical." He rubbed her shoulders.
>
> "I don't put people on pedestals. Everyone blows it from time to time." Especially her.

Is Dani right? Can good people—folks with pure motives, sincerity, and integrity—actually fall that far and become betrayers? Or are those who commit betrayal secretly bad people? Jeremiah 9 speaks to this.

7. Psalm 91:2, 62:8, 37:3, 9:10, 118:9, 37:5, and Proverbs 3:5 all say basically the same thing. What is that? How should that make you feel about people who lie about you, strike out against you, or betray you?

8. The American proverb, "Fool me once, shame on you. Fool me twice, shame on me," basically says that people only have one chance. Once they err, they should never be trusted again. Does this work with grace? Use Mark 11:25-26, Matthew 6:12-15, Luke 11:4, Matthew 18:35, 21-22, 2 Corinthians 2:7, and Luke 23:34 to help you answer.

9. Dani attempts to read through II Timothy 1 to prepare for the Bible study that she wants to

do. But she stumbles on verse 7. I used the KJV for this verse because of its word choice: "and of a sound mind." That speaks to me of keeping my mind focused, clear, and my thoughts accurate. Check out the different translations on Bible Hub. Which of the translations do you prefer of this verse? How does it speak to your spirit?

10. Just for fun. Psychology, analyzing characters more than real people, is a hobby. What type of man is Jay? What are his weaknesses and strengths? In what areas are you hoping that he grows? (Feel free to leave your answers on my discussion page at Marji Laine.com. I'll get an automatic email, and I'd love to have a discussion with you!)

11. But don't leave Dani hanging. What type of woman is she? What are her weaknesses and strengths? And how do you hope she'll grow. (Again, share your thoughts!)

12. Finally, do Dani and Jay make a good couple? Is there a strong chance for lasting love, or do you look at their interaction and think, "I give it six months"? (Oh, yes! I've done that before with books and movies!)

About Marji

Marji Laine writes about hope and redemption. Her characters, tangled in desperate situations, rely on authentic faith in God to carry them through treachery, betrayal, and impossible circumstances.

A "graduated" homeschooling mom of four, she now teaches a high school Bible study and aspiring authors at various workshops and writing conferences. She spends most of her time formatting and designing books for Write Integrity Press. She also helps those through Roaring Lambs Ministry tell their stories.

Living with her sweet hubby of 33 years and her two rescue dogs, Marji loves her jobs – loves writing, formatting, and building covers. But given the choice, she'd rather be laughing, playing games, or doing projects with her family where one-liners are a norm. While she enjoys recharging on her own, she loves being a little goofy with her kids and their friends or acting and singing from time to time on stage.

Content is probably the best description of me. I teach my kids to "enjoy where they are while they're there." A lesson in joy that I had to learn the hard way.

She prefers mountains to beaches, dogs to cats, entrees to desserts, and Jaguars to any other vehicle. Her favorites include emerald green, autumn, stargazer lilies and white roses, New York style pizza, and red velvet cake with cream cheese icing.

You can keep up with Marji by joining her monthly newsletter list at her website, www.MarjiLaine.com. And you can also find her at the WriteIntegrity.com website as well as on her Facebook Page.

Grime Beat

Dear Reader,

Thank you so much for investing your time in my novella. My greatest hope is, through Dani and Jay's story, you will glean a nugget of truth about life and the amazing God who lavishes His love on us.

The goal for my writing is to encourage readers to cling to the excitement they had when their love for Christ was brand new. I've needed to have mine reignited at times. May my characters and their stories encourage the same action. Ours is not so much a religion as it is a personal relationship with the Lord of Lords. And like any relationship, it needs and deserves our attention.

I'm praying for you dear reader, that your heart will be touched and your spirit strengthened.

If you enjoyed *Grime Beat*, I hope that you will return to its Amazon page and leave a review. Twenty-five words (and hopefully five stars) are the nicest things anyone can give to an author.

Some wonderful folks assisted me on this, my first solo-flight into publication. I can't thank my critique partners enough. Jennifer Slattery and Carole Towriss trudged through my first draft. I feel like I owe them both a pair of shoes. Patricia Pacjac Carroll and Jackie Castle worked through some concept changes. Their insight with indie publication has been invaluable. Then Christa Upton, proofreader extraordinaire, offered her services and made this story shine. A couple of professionals assisted me with my details. I'm indebted to a Dallas Police Officer and a Dallas Fireman, but I won't mention names, just in case I made a mistake. I wouldn't want them to get teased for my misunderstanding! And for my recreated covers, I owe thanks to Chautona Having. Without her vision and suggestions, I'd still be working on them!

My family has been encouraging! Dear Boy and Sweet Hubby gave me boosts just when I needed them. Precious Redhead was always willing to read over sections to make sure they made sense. And my Dinky Twinkies are the most encouraging cheerleaders an author could have. DT #1 has endured hours of What-if scenarios and plot-outlining. And DT #2 is my greatest Facebook fan, always liking and sharing every post. They both give the best hugs and fuss at me when I start to get down on myself. I'm so blessed that even as teenagers, they can exhibit love with such abandon!

Finally, I want to thank my Savior for giving me His words. May I be faithful with those for as long as He chooses to share them with me.

Until next time, dear reader!

Be Blessed!

Marji

PS. Come visit with me at
MarjiLaine.com!

Grime Fighter Mysteries
A Complete Series!

Working as a crime scene cleaner is perfect for neat-nick Dani Foster who has recently been relocated by her witness security contact. But she can't hide the investigative reactions drilled into her by her detective father. Even though her discoveries, and the explorations they instigate, often put her into funny, uncomfortable, and sometimes dangerous positions.

COUNTER POINT
Book 1 of *Heath's Point Suspense*

Her dad's gone. Her business is in trouble, and her car's in the lake. Cat McPHerson doesn't have anything else to lose... except her life. And a madman is determined to take that.

Her former boyfriend, Ray Alexander, returns as a hero from his foreign mission, bringing back souvenirs in the form of death-threats. Cat must find a way to trust Ray, the man who broke her heart or neither of them will survive.

BREAKING POINT
Book 2 of *Heath's Point Suspense*

Why would anyone want her dead?

Alynne Stone wanted nothing to do with her parents' inn after they left their lifelong home in Dallas to move to Heath's Point, Texas. Then an emergency phone call not only drew her to her parents' bed and breakfast, it thrust her into the crosshairs of a killer.

Lieutenant Jason Danvers has no idea why his kind and generous friend was killed. But the man's beautiful, prodigal daughter needs all the help he can give her to stay alive.

AIN'T MISBEHAVING

Book 1 of the
Dallas Duets Clean Billionaire Romance Series

Annalee Chambers: Poised, wealthy, socially elite. Convict.

She floated through life in a pampered, crystal bubble until she smashed it with a single word. Dealing with the repercussions of that word might break her, ruin her family, and land her in jail. That is, unless a handsome worker from the "other" side of the tracks, who has secrets of his own, can help her find her way.